"How Long Were You Going To Wait Before Telling Me?" He Demanded, His Voice Like Velvet Over Steel.

She decided to try to bluff him out, then abruptly changed tack, choosing to attack him on his own terms. "I could ask you the same thing. How long were you going to wait before telling me you'd bought this building? I never stood a chance to buy out, did I?"

"You would have known in good time, Blair. Now, it is not like you to be unwell, and I assume it can be due to only one thing. So, I will ask you again. How long were you going to wait before telling me you were pregnant?"

"Until never!"

"Wrong answer."

He covered the short distance between them in the blink of an eye. One arm curved around her back, holding her captive against his body. And darn it, her body responded instantly to his touch.

Dear Reader,

Family. Responsibility. Honor.

For some people these are the cornerstones of their lives, and so it is for Draco Sandrelli and for Blair Carson, although for totally different reasons.

I'm always fascinated when I look at what drives people to do the things they do, to strive for the goals they want to achieve. I'm always looking for the core belief that makes them want that goal so very much. Blair Carson is one of those driven people—but is her goal really what *she* wants?

In *Secret Baby, Public Affair,* Draco and Blair have to learn to balance the needs that drive them with what they really want. Can an intensely proud and aristocratic man and an equally proud and goal-driven woman find a common ground before it's too late for them both?

I hope you love reading this second installment in my ROGUE DIAMONDS trilogy as much as I enjoyed developing it and bringing it to you.

In closing, I'd like to thank Josie Caporetto for her generous help with all matters Tuscan. Any mistakes are my own.

With warmest wishes,

Yvonne Lindsay

YVONNE LINDSAY

SECRET BABY, PUBLIC AFFAIR

Published by Silhouette Books
America's Publisher of Contemporary Romance

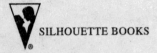

SILHOUETTE BOOKS

ISBN-13: 978-0-373-76930-8
ISBN-10:   0-373-76930-X

SECRET BABY, PUBLIC AFFAIR

Visit Silhouette Books at www.eHarlequin.com

Printed in U.S.A.

Books by Yvonne Lindsay

Silhouette Desire

The Boss's Christmas Seduction #1758
The CEO's Contract Bride #1776
The Tycoon's Hidden Heir #1788
Rosselini's Revenge Affair #1811
Tycoon's Valentine Vendetta #1854
Jealousy & a Jewelled Proposition #1873
Claiming His Runaway Bride #1890
†*Convenient Marriage, Inconvenient Husband* #1923
†*Secret Baby, Public Affair* #1930

*New Zealand Knights
†Rogue Diamonds

YVONNE LINDSAY

New Zealand born to Dutch immigrant parents, Yvonne Lindsay became an avid romance reader at the age of thirteen. Now, married to her "blind date" and with two surprisingly amenable teenagers, she remains a firm believer in the power of romance. Yvonne feels privileged to be able to bring to her readers the stories of her heart. In her spare time, when not writing, she can be found with her nose firmly in a book, reliving the power of love in all walks of life. She can be contacted via her Web site, www.yvonnelindsay.com.

To my Mum and my (late) Dad, thank you both for always letting me pursue my imagination, my dreams and my goals and for always encouraging me to believe I could achieve or be whatever I wanted.

One

"You were comfort sex. Nothing more."

At least that was all she'd ever let him be. Blair maintained eye contact with Draco Sandrelli and prayed he'd leave before she did something stupid—like faint or throw up all over his highly polished handmade boots. Her stomach, which had been unsettled since breakfast, clenched in a completely different way as he flashed a smile at her, the one he'd used just before they'd tumbled into bed together for the first time.

"*Cara mia,* you know I am so much more than that."

His voice dripped sensuality, its sound sending a shimmer of heat through her. She still woke in the night remembering the sound of him, as rich as the rolling timbre of distant thunder on an electrically charged, storm-tossed evening. And worse, remembering the feel of him, the sensation of his body against hers—inside hers. She fought back the small sound that rose in her throat—a sound driven by the heat that suffused her body and insinuated itself along her nerve endings in curling tendrils of desire.

The gold flecks in Draco's green eyes glinted as he watched her reaction. For someone she'd barely met, he seemed able to read her like a book. A tiny smile played around the sensual curve of his lips. He hadn't even forgone his usual designer stubble for today's memorial service, although he'd slicked back his glossy dark hair off his almost too perfect face, its length finishing in a ducktail at his nape. On any other man the style would look ridiculous, but on Draco… Blair swallowed against the sudden dryness in her mouth.

Really, for a man he was too beautiful to be classed as handsome, but despite her reasoning her pulse still raced to a tribal beat.

"Have dinner with me tonight," he coaxed.

"No. No way. I mean it, Draco. Call what we had a holiday fling, whatever. It's not happening again. I'm home now and back at work. Which reminds me, I have things to attend to and I'm sure you do too."

No matter what, she wasn't going to ask him what he was doing here. After all, what were the odds that her uncharacteristic holiday indulgence would turn up at Ashurst Collegiate today? Especially at the memorial reception she'd agreed to do as a favor for one of her dad's oldest friends. As tempting as it was to indulge in another forbidden delight with the sole heir to the Sandrelli empire, Blair had more important things on her mind.

She summoned every ounce of self-control in her arsenal and, tipping her nose ever so slightly in the air, spun on her heel and stalked away.

She sensed, rather than heard, the moment he decided to follow her—the fine hairs on the back of her neck prickling to attention. Blair increased her pace, turned a corner in the corridor and slipped through the doorway leading into the voluminous kitchen off Jubilee Hall, where the reception was being held. She flattened herself against the wall and fought to control her hammering heartbeat, hoping like mad he hadn't seen her duck in here.

Even her hands were trembling, she realized. She hadn't been this upset since she'd caught her fiancé, Rhys, and her best friend, Alicia, in the wine cellar of the converted villa that housed Carson's, her restaurant. The pain of losing the man she'd planned her future with to the friend who was supposed to have stood beside her in the church only a few days later had been unspeakable. Their joint betrayal still stung with the sharpness of a stingray's barb.

It was what had led her to her flight to Italy and tour of Tuscany, and ultimately to Draco Sandrelli, where she'd promptly fallen under his seductive spell.

Yes, he was comfort sex all right. Totally addictive, mind-blowingly generous comfort sex. And just what she'd needed to rebuild her flagging self-esteem. Nothing more.

She shoved herself off the wall and carried on through the kitchen, mentally checking off what she needed to do before returning to Carson's and preparing for her night's clientele. She was relieved to see her personal tools of the trade had been neatly packed back into the case she'd brought them in—a quick check ensured everything was where it should be. There was nothing further for her to do. The casual crew she'd hired to work the reception would complete the cleanup and return the crockery to the restaurant in a couple of hours' time.

Blair smoothed her hands over her uniform, the tailored, crisp short-sleeved white blouse and black skirt which neatly hugged her slim hips, drawing strength from the familiarity of its texture.

She hitched the box against her hip and carried it through the kitchen to the back door and walked around on the graveled drive to where she'd parked her station wagon. She eyed the paint work on her old workhorse with a critical eye. If she hadn't taken the trip to Tuscany she could have replaced old Gertie here with a new vehicle. But if she'd done that she would have remained a victim to Rhys and Alicia's perfidy, instead of learning more about the woman she could be. About the woman she had been.

And it had been that very discovery that had taught Blair she couldn't have it all. She wasn't the kind of person who could develop an award-winning business and be a devoted life partner to anyone. No. She was happy with her decision. Work would be her life for now. And as for Draco, well, everyone was entitled to a "Draco" in their life at one time or another, she rationalized. The intensity of their affair had burned so bright and fierce, it would have totally consumed her had she stayed any longer with him. That one certain truth had made her put everything into perspective. She'd seen it happen to her father over and over, each time destroying his inner self a little more, and she'd sworn she would never succumb to such obsession.

Her wake-up call had come one morning as she'd stirred in Draco's arms, their sheets in a tangle about their naked, sated bodies, and she realized that she hadn't so much as thought about Carson's in three whole days. The realization was sobering. She'd embraced her affair with Draco with the level of passion she usually reserved solely for her work.

No, there definitely wasn't room for both a grand love and a career in her life. Her work was everything. Its success was what defined her, not something as ephemeral as physical attraction between consenting adults.

Blair had risen from their bed and packed immediately, turning a deaf ear to Draco's enticement to stay longer. As sinfully delightful as her time with Draco had been, it wasn't the kind of temptation one could build a future on. There was no security in incendiary attraction. She knew that from both her father's painful past and her own.

There was only one thing she wanted right now, and that was to see Carson's make the five-star review page of *Fine Dining* magazine. It had been her father's dream, until ill health had forced him to hand the reins of the restaurant over to Blair as he reluctantly settled into early retirement. Now it was her dream. One she thought she'd achieve with Rhys and Alicia by her side. But she could do it on her own. Carson's would become Auckland's leading restaurant. And she'd forget all about Draco Sandrelli.

Draco hesitated outside the door to the kitchen. He'd prowled the corridor in frustration, after finding no sign of Blair. She had to be in here. Unconsciously, he straightened his shoulders. They needed to talk and he wasn't taking no for an answer. When Blair had left his bed that morning he had been prepared to move mountains to get her to stay. It had only been the urgent call to his parents' home, situated a few kilometers away within the Sandrelli estate, that had stopped him. Of course, by the time he'd returned from his father's sickbed, Blair had left the palazzo, leaving no forwarding address.

Seeing her here today had taken him by surprise, but he wasn't the kind of man who looked a gift horse in the mouth. This was a second chance. The magnetism between them had been instant, and he knew better than most that that kind of draw did not happen between couples every lifetime. Too many people settled for what was expected of them—for second best. He'd done that very thing once, out of honor and respect for his family and his dead brother, but the result had been catastrophic. He would not do that again.

The attraction was too fierce.

He settled his hand on the swing door into the kitchen and entered just in time to see Blair exiting at the far end of the room. Draco's strides ate up the distance between them and he burst through the back entrance just as

Blair loaded a case into the back of the barely roadworthy vehicle in front of her.

"Blair."

"I've said all I have to say, Draco," she sighed, as she unlocked the driver's door and slid in behind the wheel.

Draco stopped her as she tried to swing her door shut.

"Ah yes, but you haven't listened yet to what I have to say."

"To be frank, I'm really not interested in what you have to say."

She tried to wrestle the door closed, and gave up with an angry huff of air when that proved impossible. She crossed her arms defensively over her stomach and stared fixedly out the windshield.

"What's the matter, Draco, can't you tolerate someone turning you down? Granted, I'm sure it probably hasn't happened often in your lifetime, but surely you can get used to it just this once," she snapped.

He smiled in response to her rancor. She sounded like a spitting kitten all in a temper.

"I just want to talk. You left so suddenly. We never had a chance to say good-bye properly."

Draco noticed that that elicited a response. Through the thin cotton of her blouse he saw the instant her nipples peaked against the sheer fabric of her bra. A bra he knew she wore more as a concession to her position at work than out of necessity. He loved her small, high breasts. Loved the way he could elicit a screaming response from her just by nipping ever so gently at their rose-pink tips. He'd never known a woman so sensitive in that area. Never enjoyed one as much as he had Blair. And he wanted to do it all again. And again.

Blair looked up, catching his gaze that was firmly riveted on her breasts.

"Oh, for goodness' sake." She reached forward to twist her keys in the ignition. "We've said all we have to say. Or at least I have. Like I said before, you were a holiday fling. Good in bed and good for my ego. But that's it. What we had is finished. Now please, let go of my car door before I have to call security."

"Now that's where I disagree, *delizia,* we are far from finished. I will let you go now, but rest assured, Blair, I will see you again and we will finish this conversation properly."

He stood back from the car and watched as she slammed the door shut without saying another word. She crashed the car into gear, and he winced at the ancient motor's protest as she floored the accelerator and spun up a rooster tail of gravel from beneath her tires.

He watched as she drove away, a grim smile of satisfaction on his face, now that the registration details of her vehicle were firmly emblazoned in his mind. She might think she'd gotten away. But his reach far exceeded his grasp and he'd find her, and have her in his bed again. Soon.

Movement over by the car park caught his attention. His best friends—Brent Colby and Adam Palmer—stood by the Moto Guzzi bikes he'd arranged to have exported to New Zealand so they could enjoy a taste of their misspent youth whenever they managed to all be in the country at the same time. They'd come a long way from the teenage maniacs who'd spent the night of their graduation dinner demon riding on the back roads near their prestigious private school, but there was nothing that beat the sensation of mastering the power of the motorbike and flying along the road.

Brent was a self-made millionaire, and if Draco hadn't already loved and respected him as much as he did, Brent would have earned that respect twice over when he'd made and then lost his fortune, only to rebuild it twenty times stronger than before. Brent's cousin, Adam, came from different stock. New Zealand old money, which, although it didn't go back as far as the Sandrelli bloodlines, could hardly be sneered at. The Palmer family was a mover and shaker in New Zealand industry, with interests spread far and wide across the globe.

Thinking about the Sandrelli bloodlines brought solemn awareness, settling like a dark cloak around his shoulders. The Sandrellis ended, or continued, with Draco, as his ailing father had pointed out to him on more than one recent occasion. The responsibility to his family history sat firmly and heavily on his shoulders alone. Which made prospects with Blair all the more interesting—if he could only get her to agree to see him again.

He jogged over to meet his friends. It was time to head back to Brent's for drinks and a few hands of cards, and on the ride back to Auckland, Draco could formulate his plan.

Blair might think she'd gotten away from him, but all she'd done was entice him all the more. Let her think she had the upper hand for now, but he knew she was no more capable of resisting him than he was of walking away from her. A man didn't get this lucky twice in his life and walk away.

The problem was, would he be able to bring his father his heart's desire before it was too late? His last stroke had been mild, but the doctors had warned that he could suffer a debilitating or fatal stroke at any time.

Draco would just have to make certain he wasn't too late. Sandrellis had dominated the countryside around the palazzo for centuries. And even though the mantle of succession had fallen by default onto his shoulders with the death of his brother ten years ago, he would not be the one who saw to their end. His union with Blair Carson would provide the grandchildren demanded by his parents—and if their incendiary attraction was anything to go by, it would be no hardship to do so.

Neither Brent nor Adam spoke as he came to a halt beside his motorbike, but the curiosity on their faces spoke volumes.

"Don't even ask," he warned as he reached for his glossy black helmet and jammed it onto his head, flipping the dark visor down over his face.

He'd tell them about Blair eventually. When he had her firmly where he wanted her.

Two

"He's here again. That makes it seven nights in a row, sweetie." Gustav, Blair's blatantly gay headwaiter smiled and raised one brow as he brought the new order to the kitchen.

Blair's knife slipped and clattered on the chopping board, narrowly missing her fingertip. She drew in a leveling breath. Draco had turned up to take a single table each night since the memorial service. He was later than usual tonight, and the anticipation of waiting and wondering whether he'd arrive, or whether he'd returned to Tuscany, had tied her stomach in knots. Her scattered attention, combined with one of her kitchen hands being off sick, had put them uncharacteristically behind schedule.

Certainly not the behavior of an award-winning chef

in an award-winning restaurant. Blair dragged her re-
calcitrant thoughts together. There was only one objective that could take priority in her mind, and Draco
Sandrelli was not that objective.

"What did he order?"

She mentally crossed her fingers and hoped it was
something she could get out quickly. Anything that
would see him leave again. Soon.

"The Scaloppine alla Boscaiola, with sautéed mixed
vegetables. For a big guy he sure eats light, maybe he
saves his appetite for other things," Gustav responded
with a slightly salacious wink before collecting an order
from under the heat lamps and swinging back through
the doors to the restaurant.

Blair allowed herself a brief sigh of relief. The
mushroom with pork escalopes dish was simple and
easy to prepare, the sautéed vegetables equally so. They
were among the many dishes she'd learned to prepare
during her culinary tour of Tuscany, the tour that had
taken an unexpected detour from the markets and
kitchens and into Draco's bed.

As Blair warmed the olive oil in a heavy pan on the
stove top she tried not to think about that detour. About
the overwhelming pull of attraction she'd felt the instant
her eyes had met his across the courtyard, as she'd
stepped off the tour bus at Palazzo Sandrelli. Nor did
she want to remember the near painful urge to belong
in a place like the palazzo, with its generation-worn
steps leading to the front entrance and its permanence
and longevity.

She and her father had lived a nomadic lifestyle after

her mother had left them. Traveling from one city to another, usually following the tourist beat of traffic in holiday seasons, to find work. Carson's had been the only thing in her life that had been a constant. It was her home, her base. And if she was to ensure its continued popularity she needed to pull her head out of the clouds and get to work, she reminded herself dourly as she added the pork slices to the pan and turned to attend to the sautéed vegetables.

It was only as she plated up the scaloppine that Blair allowed her thoughts to drift back to Draco. Each night he'd sent back compliments to the kitchen. Normally, she would have gone out into the restaurant to speak personally with her diners, but she was afraid to face him again. Afraid of her own feelings.

What if he persisted, as he'd begun to at the memorial service? What if he wanted more? Just knowing he was here under the same roof had her nerve endings singing, her skin feeling too tight for her body. Every sense within her was attuned to him, to the knowledge that, just through the swinging doors, he dined alone. And she knew he was just biding his time. Men like Draco liked to win. She'd had firsthand experience of that.

Yet still, for some strange reason she remained on tenterhooks for Draco's opinion of his meal. Like it even mattered, she scorned herself, as she carried on through the motions of completing the finishing touches on the desserts heading out to the late table of six that had just arrived.

"Blair?"

Gustav had come back through to the kitchen, mischief written all over his features.

"Please don't tell me a busload of tourists have arrived and they're all demanding the Ossibuchi," Blair countered, naming the dish that had sold out an hour ago.

"No, nothing so simple. It's Mr. Handsome. He wants to speak to you *personally*."

Blair's heart stuttered in her chest. "And you've given him my apologies, haven't you."

"No, actually. I said you'd be right out."

"Gustav!"

"Look, it's eleven-thirty, the restaurant is nearly empty, bar the dessert and coffees on table ten. You know the kitchen is under control. There's no reason why you can't go and enjoy a port with him before we close up. Go on, live a little. It's about time you had some fun."

Blair groaned inwardly. Ever since she'd broken her engagement to Rhys and summarily dismissed him and Alicia from their duties at Carson's—a dismissal that had cost her dearly afterwards when their employment lawyer had pointed out she hadn't followed due process—Gustav had been after her to lighten up and socialize.

If only he knew, she thought. She'd already had about all the fun she could handle. It was why she had thrown herself back into work as soon as she'd stepped off the plane a few weeks ago.

Gustav yanked on her apron strings and snatched the heavy linen swathe from her narrow hips, then handed her the lipstick she kept in a drawer near the swinging doors for those moments she went out to circulate amongst diners.

"Go on. It won't kill you. Look, honey, if I thought I stood a chance I'd be at that table pronto, but he's made it clear he wants you."

Reluctantly, Blair took the lipstick and swiped it across her lips.

"There, satisfied?" she said, challenging him.

"Not hardly, sweetie." He reached up and swiped the net she wore over her hair off her head and tousled her hair into a fluffy mess. "Now I'm satisfied."

Gustav took her by the shoulders, spun her around and pushed her in the direction of the restaurant.

"Don't worry about the kitchen. We'll take care of everything. You just enjoy yourself."

As the door swung closed behind her, Blair could swear she heard the faint sound of applause from her staff. A swift glance over her shoulder through the porthole-shaped window showed Gustav taking a bow. Blair fought back a smile as she turned her attention back to the man waiting on the secluded table set in the deep bay window of the old villa.

Draco rose as Blair walked toward him. For a while, he'd wondered if his waiter had been leading him on, saying that Blair would join him for an after-dinner drink, but here she was. Finally.

He raked his gaze over her, taking in the weariness that tightened the lines of her angular face. Not classically beautiful, certainly, but the sweeping arc of her slender, dark brows over eyes the color of dark chocolate, and the long straight line of her nose, lent character to a face that might otherwise be ordinary.

She walked with the grace of the naturally slender, the bulky chef's jacket over baggy checkered pants— the standard kitchen uniform here in New Zealand— hiding the long, lean strength of her body and the perfectly shaped breasts he'd bet even now were tipped with rose peaks. A sudden flush spread across her high cheekbones and her eyes glowed with the flame of heat that he knew answered his own.

Deep inside him he felt the thrum of anticipation begin to build. By the end of the night she'd be in his bed. He knew it as well as he knew the contours of her body. And he could barely wait to feel her beneath him again. They had unfinished business to resolve between them. Blair Carson would learn she couldn't run away from him and not expect him to follow.

His feral instincts wanted nothing more than to take her by the hand and lead her straight out the front door to his waiting car. To whisk her away to his Viaduct Basin apartment in the city and bare her to his gaze, to his hunger. And then to sate them both.

A fine tremor ran through his body as he fought back the urge to do just that. As she neared his table she displayed all the characteristics of a gazelle poised for flight. The last thing he wanted to do right now was scare her off. She'd run from him once before; it was up to him to ensure she wouldn't do so again.

She lifted her hand to him as she drew to a halt beside the table.

"I trust you enjoyed your meal, Mr. Sandrelli."

Draco let his lips relax into a smile, watching her pupils dilate in reaction, and her lips firm, as she read his humor at her attempt to keep things between them strictly on a business footing.

He took her hand and pulled her toward him, kissing her briefly on each cheek in traditional European style before releasing her hand and gesturing for her to take the seat adjacent to his.

"I always enjoy the fruits of your toil, Blair. Your cleverness in the kitchen is only surpassed by your—"

"Perhaps I can get you a drink. Gustav mentioned port. Is that your preference?" She wheeled away from the table but he reached out and snagged her hand.

"Stay, Gustav will bring us our drinks shortly. I wanted a little time with you first, just to talk."

"If that's what you want," Blair answered begrudgingly.

"You learned well during your time in Tuscany. The dish you served tonight, that was from your stay in Lucca, *si?*"

"Yes, I've incorporated a few of the recipes from the region into our menu. They've been popular."

"And you've been busy. You look tired." He reached across the table and brushed the pad of his thumb gently across the bluish tint to the skin beneath her eyes.

She flinched, breaking the tenuous contact almost as soon as it had begun.

"It's all good. It's what I want."

Ah, here it came. Her not-so-subtle wall of defense.

"But everyone needs some respite in their life from time to time. Tell me, *cara mia,* what do you do to unwind—to relax?"

"I've just come back from holiday, Draco. I don't need to relax."

He snorted inelegantly. "Holiday? Blair, you worked your way through that culinary tour. You can hardly call that a holiday. Except for—"

"Ah, here's our port." Blair interrupted him again, taking the two cut-crystal glasses from the silver tray Gustav held in one hand and dismissing him with a look. "Here, *salute!*"

Draco accepted the glass from her and set it down on the table in front of him. He could see straight through her. She thought if she could get him to drink his port, their conversation would be over, and he'd be gone. How wrong she was. When he left here tonight, she would be with him. Willingly.

He played with the stem of the glass, admiring the quality of the crystal. She didn't stint on anything here in the restaurant. From the fittings and furnishings to the tableware and service—it was all of the highest quality. Yes, Blair Carson took her passions seriously. And he liked that about her. A lot.

She took a sip of her port, the fortified liquid leaving a sheen on her lips. His fingers tightened reflexively as the tip of her tongue swept across her lips to remove the residual alcohol. He ached for her to take another sip, so he could lean forward and taste the port on her lips, on her tongue.

Her next words came as a surprise.

"What do you want from me Draco? What will it take to make you go away?"

He leaned back in his seat, shifting his hips slightly to ease the ache that had built low in his groin.

"What makes you think I will go away?"

She shook her head. "We both know your business demands will take you home soon. Already you've been here, what, a week? I imagine you'll need to be leaving soon, I just want to know what I can do to make it sooner."

"Come home with me."

"To the palazzo? You have to be joking."

Ultimately, yes, that was his goal. To have her back where she belonged, with him. But in the meantime he would be satisfied with small victories.

"Tonight. To my apartment."

He leaned forward again and lifted her hand with his, dragging her fingertips gently across his lips. He felt the shudder of awareness course through her. The fire between them still burned bright and fierce.

"Just tonight?" her voice shook ever so slightly. "And then you'll leave me alone?"

It was a start. He inclined his head. "I've missed you, Blair. Let me show you how much."

"I—I don't know."

"I'm not a man to beg, *cara mia,* but I beg of you now. You cannot fight this thing between us. Even you have to admit what we have is something rare, something special. Not even with your Rhys did you share this, no?"

Her fingers flexed in his and he knew he had her. For tonight at least.

"All right. Tonight only. I'll need to get a few things."

"Certainly. Bring as much as you want. Stay longer."

She withdrew her hand from his clasp. "No. It will only be tonight. Give me your address and I'll bring my car."

"That won't be necessary. I have a car and driver at my disposal. Where do we go to pick up your things."

Draco was on his feet and helping Blair to hers before she could rethink things and change her mind.

"Upstairs, I have a couple of rooms upstairs. The stairs are around the back through the kitchen."

"Then I shall wait for you here."

He leaned forward and brushed the lightest touch of his lips against hers. He knew he shouldn't have done it the second he felt her breath against his lips. What was supposed to have been a simple caress sent a flare of heat through his body, and instead of withdrawing from her, as he'd planned, his hand snaked up the slender column of her neck, his fingers tangling in the short strands of her hair so he could angle her head better to plunder the softness of her mouth. Her lips parted with a soft moan, her tongue darting to meet his. The taste of her was intoxicating, sending his blood to thrum through his body with a pagan beat.

It had been like this the first time he'd touched her. This all-consuming need to have more of her. To take what she had to offer and give back threefold in return. He'd never known such consuming passion, not even with Marcella. The thought was both sobering and enticing at the same time.

Blair's uninhibited response gave him all the answer he needed. He'd been right to pursue her, right to bide his time before making his move. She was as affected by their magnetism as he. Being here each night and not contacting her, not touching her, had been a master plan. As calculated as it sounded, it had been the only way to show her that this thing between them couldn't be ignored, but was there to be indulged in.

Dio! He couldn't get enough of her. He nipped lightly at her lower lip, suckling against the pliant tissue, absorbing the tiny sound of pleasure that emanated from deep in her throat.

The clatter of cutlery on bowls brought him suddenly to his senses and he pulled back, his fingers stroking the satin softness of her neck one last time before he forced himself to let her go.

"Hurry. I don't want to waste a moment," he said, his voice pitched low so only Blair could hear him.

For a second she wavered, as if slightly off balance. Truth be told, he felt much the same way. But then, with a slight nod, she walked away from him, her steps brisk and to the point.

Three

"Is it getting hot in here, or is it just you?" Gustav remarked, fanning himself theatrically, as Blair pushed through the kitchen doors and headed straight toward the back door.

"Can it, Gus. You got what you wanted."

"Well, technically, no. But it sure looks like you're going to. Way to go, Blair. It's about time. And don't worry about the restaurant. I'll lock up."

Blair hesitated, her hand on the back door. "What do you mean, it's about time?"

"Well, you know. Since that whole business with Rhys and Alicia, it's like all your enthusiasm for the place got sucked out of you."

Had she really been so transparent? Granted, the breakup with Rhys over his betrayal with Alicia and the subsequent legal battle over severing their employment had been draining, but she hadn't for a minute thought she'd let that impact on her work, or the workplace.

Gustav carried on. "Since you came back from Italy, it's as if you have a new vibrancy about you, and it shows in your food and everything. Everyone here is much happier. It's good. And quite frankly, if this guy is the one that made you like this, then all kudos to him. He is the one, isn't he? The one you met while you were away?"

"Yeah, he is. You don't think I'm making a mistake, do you?"

"Mistake? You have to be kidding me! Get yourself out of here before I take him off you."

"Thanks, I owe you." Blair pushed open the back door and shot up the back staircase to the compact flat she called home when she wasn't working.

She grabbed a backpack from the tiny hall closet and shoved toiletries and a change of clothes inside, then quickly divested herself of her work gear. She wrinkled her nose as she dragged on a long-sleeved T-shirt and a soft cotton skirt with an asymmetrical hemline. Then she shoved her feet into pretty, low-heeled sandals. She would have appreciated time to grab a quick shower, to rid herself of the lingering aromas of the kitchen, but she had the feeling that Draco would be dragging her still wet into the car if she kept him waiting too much longer.

A pang of need arrowed through her center. One kiss. That was all it had taken and she'd been lost to him. Lost to the sensual delight he promised with every touch of his skillful fingers, every taste of his practiced tongue.

She quickly switched off the lights and locked the

door behind her, her sandals clattering on the wooden stairs as she returned to the restaurant. To Draco.

He pushed back from the table and stood the second she entered the dining room. Butterflies danced to a crazy beat in her stomach. Was she doing the right thing? Gus seemed to think so. Draco definitely thought so. But wasn't she just setting herself up for failure? She knew how hot the flame between her and Draco had burned back in Italy. She'd left before there could be any lasting damage. By agreeing to spend this night with him, would she end up scorched and regretful? Worse, would she be able to walk away from him come morning?

He didn't give her time to think. In one instant he had taken her arm to guide her outside, in the next they were seated on the leather backseat of the limousine that had edged forward at the curbside the instant he'd set foot outside Carson's. Every nerve ending in Blair's body was on full alert, attuned to the leashed power and strength of the man seated beside her.

Draco uttered a clipped command in Italian. The limousine driver closed the smoked glass divider between them and pulled smoothly away, gliding into the late-night traffic on Ponsonby Road.

Blair reached across the space between them, and trailed her fingertips across the expensive woven fabric encasing Draco's legs. The muscles in his thigh tensed beneath her feather-light touch.

"Don't." His voice was strangled, tight. The single word forced between rigid lips. "If you touch me now I won't be able to hold myself back, and I promised myself I would wait until we reached my apartment."

Blair's breath caught in her chest and a coil of anticipation tightened low in her belly. She lifted her hand and laid it back in her lap, her eyes seeking his in the darkened compartment of the car. The knowledge that she could affect him so deeply was empowering. While it was true that the strength of her feelings for him had terrified her, had driven her from his bed and his home and sent her on the arduous and long plane journey home from Europe, right now she was afraid of nothing.

The trip from Carson's to the Viaduct Basin took only ten minutes, and as they pulled into the parking area of the apartment building Blair acknowledged she couldn't wait another moment to be alone with Draco.

His driver came around to her door and held it open for her. As she alighted she heard the two men hold a brief discussion in Italian before the driver cruised away into the night.

A trickle of unease shimmered down her spine as she stood in the portico to the high-rise waterfront apartment complex. What the hell was she thinking? A week ago she'd told Draco he'd been nothing more than comfort sex, a couple of weeks before that she'd walked away from him, determined not to succumb to his seductive spell—and yet, here she was on the point of going to bed with him again. A shiver of something else coursed through her. Something that had nothing to do with nerves and everything to do with the visceral look of intent on the face of the man walking toward her.

Still, he didn't touch her. Instead, he picked up her pack from where the driver had deposited it and headed for the door. Blair followed, slightly cowed by his silence. Was he having second thoughts?

All the way up to his penthouse apartment she sensed the heat of his gaze. Briefly, she lifted her eyes to meet his, only to swallow convulsively when faced with the naked desire reflected in their emerald depths.

The doors swooshed open and Blair followed Draco down the heavily carpeted corridor, to the set of double doors at the end. With the swipe of a key card he opened the doors and stood aside, motioning for her to enter.

Her heels clicked on the parquet floor of the entrance, their sound masking Draco's footsteps as he closed in behind her. The muffled sound of her pack landing on the floor was all the warning she had before she was consumed by a broad band of heat at her back. Strong arms wrapped around her. Draco's mouth, hot and wet, descended onto the curve of her neck, his tongue tracing a sensual line up to her ear. The hard swell of his erection pressed against her buttocks and she squirmed, her action wringing a harsh groan from his throat.

He spun her around to face him, his thigh wedging between her legs with delicious friction, to rub against that part of her that flamed, begging for his touch. Blair's back flattened against the paneled wall behind her and she lifted her arms to Draco's shoulders before tangling her fingers in his hair and dragging his mouth down to hers.

Suddenly all the hunger she'd held at bay for the past few weeks erupted beneath the onslaught of his lips, the rasp of his tongue against hers. Time and place held no consequence, every molecule in her body focused solely on this moment, this man. One night—it would be their last but it would be the best.

Her skirt hitched up under the push of Draco's hands as he stroked up her legs, his broad palms caressing the backs of her thighs before clasping the roundness of her buttocks and pulling her hard against the demanding line of his arousal. A spiral of pleasure feathered out from her core, a promise of things to come.

It was insane, what they were doing, but Blair was incapable of sane thought or behavior any more. Draco invaded her senses, her every thought, her every desire. She shuddered anew as he dragged her panties away and cupped her, his fingers slick on her body, on the evidence of her need for him. He ground the heel of his palm against her and she cried out as the tiny rockets of pleasure sparked through her.

"Please," she begged, "please, Draco. More."

She heard her words—shamelessly wanton—as they hung in the air, and knew she could wait no longer. She fumbled for his belt, sliding the leather loose from its clasp, and then unsnapped the button before ripping down his fly. She was greedy for him now, reaching past the waistband of his silk briefs, hungry to feel his satin heat against her skin.

In the instant she loosed him from the confines of his briefs he hitched her higher against the wall and hooked her legs high over his hips. He pulled a condom from his pocket before his pants slid down his legs and quickly sheathed himself. Blair reached between them to guide his hardness to her entrance and then with one deep thrust they were one. She gripped his shoulders as he surged within her, driving her closer and closer to her peak. And then, in a mad rush of sensation, she was there. Her body clenching and convulsing around him, her hands digging into his shoulders, her thighs tight bands around his waist. With a raw cry of triumph he joined her on the raft of pleasure that soared through them both, his body imprisoning her against the wall, his breath hard and fast, his heartbeat hammering in his chest.

Slowly Blair became aware of where they were. God, they hadn't even made it more than a few feet inside the door. At least he'd had the presence of mind to close it behind them. Her whole body trembled with aftershocks of delight, her breathing came in ragged gasps.

"It seems I'm somewhat lacking in finesse tonight," Draco said close to her ear, his voice uneven but carrying an unmistakable note of humor.

"So it would seem," Blair agreed, grazing her lips along the column of his throat and being rewarded as he flexed against her, sending yet another aftershock of pleasure to ripple through her body.

"I'll make it up to you. I promise."

"I don't know if I can take any more. That was so…so…" Words failed her.

"So cathartic?"

He was right. It had been cathartic. Despite the late hour, despite the fact she'd already been on her feet all night in a busy kitchen, she felt energized, invigorated. Suddenly, she looked forward to Draco's idea of making it up to her.

He lifted her slightly and withdrew from her body, letting her unhook her legs from his waist and slide them down to the ground. She was amazed she could even stand. Her skirt fluttered down around her thighs as she moved off the wall. Draco rearranged his clothing.

"Come, I think we both need to shower after that. Let me take care of you."

Blair picked up her backpack and let him take her by the hand as he led her through the apartment. Floor-to-ceiling glass faced the inner harbor and Viaduct Basin. Light glittered off a myriad of buildings and luxury super-yachts and cruisers moored in the basin to reflect on the inky surface of the ocean. The vista was surreal. About as surreal as the fact she'd just allowed herself to be swept away by a sensual hunger she'd only barely begun to acknowledge.

The master suite led off the living room, and beyond that, the master bathroom. Soft dove-gray walls softened the black-and-gray marble vanity tops and black-tiled floor. Blair placed her pack on the vast spread of marble as Draco reached inside the massive shower stall to turn on the water. His task complete, he turned back to face Blair. Even without the evidence of his arousal against his trousers she could tell by the look on his face that he wanted her again. He framed her face with his large hands and kissed her, softly this time, taking his time to play the soft tissue of her lips against his before breaking contact.

His hands went to the hem of her T-shirt and he lifted it up and over her head. He traced one finger along the line of the rose-pink lace of her bra, where it met the gentle swell of her breast, before bending his head to press soft warm kisses where his finger had just been.

With an expert hand he unsnapped the clasp at the back, and the fabric, which had so ably cupped her, slid away to reveal her to his avaricious gaze.

"So beautiful, so perfect," he murmured, rolling the tips of her nipples between his fingertips before bending his dark head to lave first one taut bud, then the other, with the tip of his tongue.

He reached behind her to unzip her skirt and let it fall to the floor, leaving her standing only in her sandals. He knelt before her and placed her hands on his shoulders before lifting one foot to unbuckle the strap at her ankle. Each movement was so measured, so deliberate—in total contrast to the uncontrolled passion that had consumed them both only minutes ago—and deep inside her Blair recognized the building fire and knew Draco's idea of making things up to her would be monumental.

Once she was completely naked, he swiftly divested himself of his shoes and socks before pulling his shirt off and sending his trousers and briefs to the floor.

He guided her into the shower stall, angling the multiple shower heads to course over her body before he closed the door behind them.

"Oh, that feels so good," Blair moaned as the pulsing spray jets massaged her back.

Draco just smiled as he filled his hands with shower gel then began to smooth the slick liquid over her shoulders and down her arms, then stroke his hands back up again. He repeated the movement several times before gently running his hands over her chest then down to cup and gently knead her breasts.

She'd never felt "enough" before Draco. Each of the

other men she'd been with before she'd met him had teased her about her breast size. Not in a cruel way, but enough to ensure that the taunts of her teenage years rose large and ugly in her mind. Enough to make her feel less than feminine, less than a woman. But beneath Draco's touch she had no doubt she was everything he wanted, the attention he paid to her breasts, to her tight, puckered nipples, left her in no doubt whatsoever.

He filled his hands again with the shower gel and continued his ministrations, sliding one hand down to cup her and spread her legs gently. He cleaned her with an intimacy she had never experienced with anyone else, but then Draco Sandrelli was like no other man Blair knew. And that was precisely why he both scintillated and terrified her. It would be too easy to succumb to his spell, to his lovemaking. To lose herself. No, no matter what delights he brought her—and she knew there would be many—she had to remain strong. To take what he offered tonight and then go back to the life she'd chosen.

A ripple of pleasure spread from her core, just a hint of what his touch promised, she knew. His hands slid around to her buttocks, softly squeezing them before running down the backs of her thighs. He dropped to his knees, his hands still running up and down the length of her legs, and she marveled she could even stand when he brought his mouth to the apex of her thighs and pressed his lips to the sensitive bundle of nerve endings there.

His tongue flicked over the nub, at first soft then more insistent. Blair knotted her fingers in his hair, holding him to her as he increased pressure, then teasingly slowed again. Her legs were trembling, barely able to hold her slight weight when he began to suckle at her. She let her head drop back as the scream of pleasure ejected from her in tune to the orgasm that nearly rent her apart.

Draco stood, supporting Blair's quaking body with the strength of his, relishing that he could bring her so much pleasure, so much passion. For a woman who kept herself locked down so tight emotionally, he'd been ecstatic to discover the deeply hidden sensuality inside her. It was a waste for her to pour all that passion purely into her work, when she could have so much more if she would only embrace it.

He turned off the shower faucets and scooped Blair into his arms. She was so slender it was as if he lifted a child—she'd lost weight since her return to New Zealand. Weight, in his opinion, she could ill afford to lose. If he'd gauged her correctly, she'd no doubt been running herself ragged since leaving him. And if he didn't miss his mark, she was already on the point of exhaustion—her physical reaction to their lovemaking already leaving her limp, shattered in his arms.

He wrapped her in a thick, dove-gray towel and dried her with painstaking care.

"Draco?"

Her voice made him look up from his ministrations.

"Hmm?" he answered, reaching for a fresh towel to dry her hair before skimming his own body dry.

"What about you?"

He smiled. "Later. For now, you rest, *si*?"

"I'm sorry, I—"

He put a fingertip to her lips. "Don't. Don't tell me you're sorry."

He guided her to the master bedroom and pulled back the voluminous, down-filled duvet and the crisp cotton sheet before gently pushing her down onto the mattress. She was asleep in moments, confirming his belief she'd been pushing herself too hard. It was certainly more than the languor of the aftermath of love-making that dragged her into somnolence. He tossed her damp towel to one corner of the room and climbed into the bed next to her, propping himself up slightly so he could watch her as she settled into a deeper sleep. Eventually, he flipped the control that dimmed the bedroom lights into darkness and settled down onto his pillow, scooping Blair against his body and pulling the sheet over them both before letting sleep claim him also.

It was her feather-light touch that woke him only a couple of hours later. Somewhere in the night she'd slid from his hold and he'd rolled onto his stomach, a position that was becoming increasingly uncomfortable as awareness flooded his body.

Blair knelt over him. Her fingers touching, yet almost not, as they traced a line up from his ankles to the backs of his knees and then higher. Blood surged to his groin as her touch coasted up the inside of his thighs. Up and down and back again, each time moving a little higher, until goose bumps raised all over his skin anticipating her next move.

He felt the mattress shift, ever so slightly, as she moved, straddling his legs, keeping him captive, prone.

He could feel her firm buttocks on the backs of his thighs, feel the heat of her core against his bare skin. It was both a torment and a pleasure.

Her touch strengthened now, deepened as she stroked the long line of muscles on either side of his spine, stopping every now and then to change her touch to that feather-soft caress that threatened to drive him crazy with want. His hands, shoved deep under his pillow, clenched into fists as he fought not to reach for her, to spin her beneath him and torture her as she now did him.

"Are you awake yet?"

The teasing note in her voice made his lips pull into a smile.

"Yes, I am awake," he ground out through clenched teeth as her fingers tracked his spine—down, down, until she skimmed the crease of his buttocks.

He felt her weight lift from his legs.

"You'd better turn over then," she instructed.

Draco rolled over, hissing in a breath as she wrapped her fingers around his hardened length and caressed him, her other hand reaching for the packet she'd already removed from the bedside cabinet. He nearly lost it as he watched her tear the foil open with her teeth and slide the condom from its wrapper, then meticulously slide it over him.

He reached for her hips as she rose above him, poised at his tip.

"Let me," she whispered, placing her hands over his. "Let me look after you this time."

He was unused to surrendering control, whether it was in the boardroom or the bedroom, but for Blair he would do this. Her heat threatened to consume him as she lowered herself to take only his tip within her body. Every instinct within him demanded he take charge, insisted he drive into her and bring them both to the shattering pleasure he knew lay in store, but he beat back the urge and forced himself to concede.

A groan broke from his throat as she tilted her hips, taking a little more of him, then more, until finally he was exactly where he wanted to be, needed to be. She clenched her inner muscles around him, holding him tight then releasing him, shifting her hips back and forth ever so slightly with each clench and release, increasing in tempo until a sheen of sweat broke out on his body and hers.

He could keep his hands from her no longer. He reached for her, his fingers closing over the small globes of her breasts, squeezing them as she thrust forward, flicking her nipples with his thumbs. And then he was lost, pleasure unleashed in waves through his body. Beyond control, he thrust upwards and was rewarded with her cry as he felt her spasm around him, again and again, her body shaking.

He supported her against his hands as she climaxed, eventually lowering her to lie over his body. Lazily he rubbed one hand up and down her back, savoring the boneless sense of completion that permeated every part of his body.

Eventually, Blair lifted herself off him and took care of the condom. A simple thing, but one no woman had ever done for him before. When she came back into the bedroom she climbed back into bed beside him and curled up against his body and Draco allowed himself to sink into sleep, secure in the knowledge she wanted him now as much as he wanted her.

Four

Blair woke to the sound of Draco moving about the room. She kept her eyes closed and focused on keeping her breathing even. She didn't want to face him. Not now. Not in the cold light of day. She'd agreed to one night, but, if she knew him, he'd want more. And he wouldn't take no for an answer.

She listened to the gentle slide of a drawer closing and then the soft sound of his bare feet on the thickly carpeted floor. She waited until the door to the bathroom was closed before opening her eyes. She wanted out of here, right now.

Yes, they'd had the most spectacular night of love-making of her life, but Draco would never let it stop there. Men like him wanted more. Needed more. With his position back at home he was expected to marry, to raise a family. He could never do that with someone like Blair, and she didn't want to be that someone anyway. She didn't have that kind of person inside her to give.

The failure with Rhys was categorical proof of that, and with her family track history—no, best not to go down that route. Besides, where would a girl like her fit in with the centuries-old traditions of Draco's life? No, it was far, far better that she make a silent retreat here and now, before he could tempt her into wanting more—wanting *him*—again.

She swept her legs off the bed, relishing the sensation of her bare feet sinking into the plush pile of the carpet. A far cry from the polished wooden floors in her small apartment, and yet another example of the differences in their lives. Blair rose from the bed, acknowledging the minor aches in her muscles. Aches which sent a flush of desire across her body as she remembered how she'd earned them.

She looked around the room for her clothing, scowling silently as she remembered that Draco had undressed her in the bathroom and she'd left her pack in there. Would she be able to slip inside and gather her things without him noticing? She doubted it. So, what did that leave? Going home wrapped in a sheet? Hardly likely, although a sense of urgency gripped her. How much longer would Draco be in the bathroom, she wondered?

She darted across the room and listened at the door, the sound of water cascading in the shower reassuring her for a moment.

There was nothing else to do but borrow something of his, she decided. She could always courier it back to him, if he even noticed it missing. She quickly rummaged through the dark cherrywood tallboy, grabbing a T-shirt and a pair of lightweight drawstring track pants. Draco was taller than she, but not by so much that the track pants would drag on the ground. She swiftly pulled the clothes on, regretting for a moment that she hadn't had a chance to grab her shoes. *Okay,* she acknowledged, *there might not be much between them in height but there certainly was in body size.* Draco's shirt hung on her like a rag, and the pants would trip her in a minute, no matter how high she hitched them to her waist. She bent to quickly roll up the legs a couple of twists and then tied the T-shirt in a knot at her lower back. *There, that was a bit better.*

But what about her feet? A quick glance in the walk-in wardrobe confirmed there was no way her narrow feet would carry off wearing a pair of Draco's running shoes or anything else in there. She'd have to forget about footwear for now and just pray she didn't have to walk too far before finding a taxi.

She stiffened as she registered the sudden silence in the bathroom behind her. Damn, he was out of the shower. She didn't have much time.

Blair shot through the apartment and let herself out the front door. She ran lightly down the corridor to the elevator and leaned on the button to call the car to the top floor, her eyes fixed on the door to Draco's apartment the whole time. When the door whooshed open behind her she jumped, and then laughed at herself for her ridiculousness. What had she been expecting? That he'd jump out from behind the elevator doors and drag her back to the apartment, hold her there as his love slave forevermore?

She rolled her eyes at her mirrored reflection in the closing doors, taking a minute to push her fingers through her hair.

One night he'd asked for. One night he'd had. It had to be enough—for both of them.

Some people might call it running away—others, well, "tactical withdrawal" were the words that immediately came to Blair's mind. If she wasn't at the apartment or the restaurant, then Draco couldn't find her, and that's just the way she wanted it. The instant Blair got back home she showered and changed into her own clothes, grateful to put on fresh underwear and to rid herself of the tingling sensation of Draco's clothing against her bare skin. All her bare skin.

She threw the clothes in a bag for dry cleaning and added them to the laundry to be picked up by their linen supply company. Then she quickly put together a few things, enough to last her a couple of days, and headed out the door.

She hadn't been to visit her father since she'd returned from Tuscany. Now seemed as good a time as any. Monday and Tuesday were supposed to be her days off, not that she usually took them, so it wasn't as if she was running away. Not really, she told herself as she threw her bag into the passenger seat of her station wagon and put the vehicle in gear. A couple of days at the beach would do her good.

As she drove down the rutted driveway toward the

house her father rented by the beach at Kaiaua, on the Seabird Coast southeast of Auckland city, she knew she'd made the right decision. Already, the soothing sounds of the sea, the cries of wheeling gulls and the soft onshore breeze began to invigorate her in a way being back at work hadn't in a long time.

She thrust open her door and loped over to the house. She ignored the two shallow stairs that led to the weathered wraparound deck and jumped the short distance, her feet landing with a muffled thud before she ran around to where she knew her father would have his French doors open to the ocean.

"Dad?" she called as she stepped inside.

A tantalizing aroma filtered through the air to tweak at her nose, and Blair instinctively followed the scent through to the compact kitchen, just beyond the airy, open living area that faced the sea.

"I thought you might turn up today," Blair Carson, Sr. commented without turning his back as Blair entered the kitchen.

"Hello to you too, Dad."

Blair smiled at his usual, taciturn nature. Not even a surprise visit could wrest a smile from his careworn features. But then she hesitated.

"What made you expect me today?"

Her dad gestured to the laptop computer open on the small kitchen table. "That."

Blair sat down at the table and focused on the screen. Even though her dad was an hour from the city now, he liked to keep a finger on the pulse of what was happening, especially in the restaurant and entertainment industries. Her heart plummeted when she identified herself and Draco in the photo. The picture showed Draco holding her fingertips to his mouth, and more damningly, showed the expression of longing on her face.

The editorial accompanying the photo was full of conjecture and innuendo about what "something new and exciting" loomed on Blair's menu. It made her feel sick to her stomach. Worse, the reporter had gone to great lengths to emphasize the title and estates that Draco would inherit on his ailing father's death, giving him a celebrity she knew he would loathe.

"I thought you'd sworn off men," her father commented dryly after she'd read the e-zine page through to its end.

"I have."

"Then what was that all about?"

"It was him."

"The one you met in Tuscany, at the palazzo? Isn't his family some kind of royalty over there?"

"Ancestral nobility, but they haven't used their title in years. But yeah," she sighed. "The very same."

"Did he follow you here?"

"No. He was at the memorial service for Mrs. Woodley. Believe me, I tried to put him off trying to see me again."

"Obviously not all that effectively." Her father turned back to the stove. "Oh well, we should see an upswing in patronage at the restaurant. Are you going to see him again?"

Blair got up from the table and helped herself to a mug from the cupboard and poured herself a coffee from the carafe her father kept constantly full. It bothered her that her father instantly thought of the advantage to Carson's. How she felt about Draco didn't enter into it.

"No. Last night was a one-time-only."

Her father turned to look her in the eye. "Really?"

"Yes, Dad. Really."

"That's a shame. You should see him again. If only because the publicity would be good for takings. Want some breakfast?"

What? Was that it? Inquisition over already? Blair could hardly believe her father had let the subject go just like that. Still, he'd equated the e-zine gossip spread with a chance to keep Carson's up there in the public eye.

"Yes, thanks. I'm starved."

Her dad laughed, the sound like wind through dry leaves in autumn. "You're always starved. About time you put some meat on that frame, young lady."

"You can talk," Blair responded with a genuine smile.

Her lean build was a direct legacy from her father. At least she assumed it was just from him. She'd never seen a picture of her mom, and her memories of her were vague—more the sensation of a brief hug here, a lingering scent of fragrance there. The trill of amused laughter. The sound of weeping late at night.

The coffee in Blair's mug left a bitter aftertaste in her mouth. What was it about Blair and her father that they couldn't find happiness in lasting love? She'd lost count of the failed relationships he'd embarked upon and then left during her childhood, let alone since her teenage years. They'd clung to one another many a time, secure in the knowledge that no matter how often others came and went they'd always have each other.

Yet, would they? Blair felt increasingly vulnerable. A heart attack had forced Blair Sr. into early retirement. In fact, it had only been her taking over his dreams and vision for Carson's that had seen him agree to withdrawing from the restaurant. He'd had to move out of Auckland as well, because he hadn't been able to stay away, or out of the kitchen, when he'd remained in town. And while he'd been happy to cover for her during her Tuscan culinary tour—a trip that was supposed to have been her honeymoon—she could see how taxing it had been for him when she'd returned.

She owed it to her dad to see his dream for Carson's—her dream as well—come true. And if she was to achieve that ever-elusive five-star ranking for the restaurant, she had to pour everything she was into making it work.

Which meant pushing last night's memories and Draco Sandrelli very firmly into her past.

Blair felt completely reenergized when she returned to her flat at midday on Wednesday. Reenergized and refocused. A call to Gustav had confirmed her father's prediction that the e-zine article would see an upswing in business. Traditionally quieter nights, Monday and Tuesday had produced far higher receipts than usual and the restaurant had operated at near capacity each night.

She hummed to herself as she skipped downstairs and checked that preparations were well underway for the evening's menu. In the tiny office off the kitchen, where she made calls to suppliers and drafted menu plans, she came to a shuddering halt. There on her seat was a dry-cleaning package. On top of it a sheet of paper with a large question mark next to the words "not yours, I presume—G."

Damn, she'd forgotten about Draco's clothes the minute she'd dispatched them to the laundry. Would he have missed them? She doubted it. What worried her most was that sending them back to him would only rouse his interest in her again.

She picked up the packet from her chair and shot back upstairs to her rooms. She'd shove it in the cupboard and deal with it another day. She wasn't up to facing Draco again.

The evening started with the usual hustle and bustle, and Blair was glad to be back in her own kitchen. As capable as she was, her father was proprietary about his space—worse so, now that his space was so limited at the beachfront bach. She swung into the ebb and flow of cooking and plating up dishes with the years of experience and pleasure she took in her work.

By the time the front door was closed to patrons and the last diner had been seen off into a taxi at the curb, Blair was ready to put her feet up. The cleanup done in the kitchen and the last of her staff off on their way home, she took a moment to sit at one of the tables and relish the silence that now reigned supreme.

A sharp hammering at the front door had her catapulting out of her chair in shock.

Who the—

She swiveled the slim-line blind that screened the glass front door to peer out into the evening gloom.

Draco. Her heart skittered in her chest.

"Let me in, Blair. We need to talk."

"We said all we have to say, Draco. One night. Remember?"

"Vividly. Do you remember too, *cara mia?* Would you like me to repeat just which were my favorite parts—I'm sure the reporter sitting in the car just behind me would be keen for all the details."

Reporter? Blair peered past Draco's dark form. There was a car pulled right up to the curb. She caught a brief glimpse of the reporter's camera through the open window. The thought of the headlines in tomorrow's gossip pages was enough to get her to open the door and usher Draco inside immediately, not quickly enough to completely avoid the sudden flash of white light as the reporter took their picture.

"Why on earth did you bring that reporter here?" Blair demanded, her hands fisted on her hips to avoid using them for any other purpose.

"You're mistaken. I did not bring him. He was already waiting here, much as there have been reporters stationed outside my apartment and following my driver from pillar to post since early Monday morning."

Draco stepped closer to her and lifted his hand to trace a finger along her cheekbone.

"You've caught some sun. Where have you been hiding the past two days?"

Blair bristled instantly. *Hiding?*

"For your information, Draco Sandrelli, I wasn't

hiding. I went to visit my father. I do that sometimes on my days off."

"I'm impressed that you take days off," Draco said, whistling softly. "According to your staff, that doesn't happen often. Some coincidence, don't you think, that you should slip out of my apartment without saying good-bye and then go incommunicado immediately after that? Looks like hiding to me."

"What you think isn't important to me. What do you want, anyway? The restaurant, as you can see, is closed."

"Hmm, what do I want? A leading question, no?"

He closed the remaining distance between them, his arms wrapping around Blair with the familiarity of lovers, his head bending to her ear. A shiver of anticipation danced down her spine as she felt his breath against her skin.

"I'll show you what I want," he growled, before his tongue licked out to tease her earlobe.

Her hands moved to his shoulders as her knees went weak, then common sense prevailed. They were in her restaurant with reporters outside. This was totally crazy.

"No, Draco. Stop, please."

The words wrung past her lips as Blair drew on every ounce of self-control she possessed to push him away.

"We can't," she continued. "Not with—"

She gestured toward the front of the restaurant and shook her head. When the heck had her life grown so complicated?

"Fine then, we will go somewhere more private. Your rooms, perhaps?"

"To talk," Blair asserted.

"If you wish."

A tiny smile pulled at Draco's lips, the sight of that sensuous curve sending a bolt of sheer longing through Blair's body. She pushed the sensation down, refusing to let her desire for him control her, and showed him through the kitchen to the back of the restaurant.

She felt the sheer presence of him at her back, like a wall of heat imprinting the length of her body. The hairs on the back of her neck tickled with awareness.

Blair went to unlock and open the back door, but Draco forestalled her action, his hand big and warm as it trapped hers against the doorknob.

"Wait just a moment. We will open it slowly to ensure none of those reporters have snuck around the back."

Blair did as he suggested, looking both ways before signaling to him that the way was clear. He followed her up the stairs to her flat. As she pushed open the front door she was suddenly assailed with the massive differences between their lives.

Draco came from wealth, a long, long line of money and privilege with a heritage that stretched back centuries. Even his apartment here in Auckland shrieked money, although the simple, modern lines were a far cry from the opulence of the palazzo. She smiled to herself. *Palazzo.* How many people could say a palazzo was their home?

Oh yeah, they were different all right. For some reason it hadn't seemed to matter when she was in Tuscany—she'd been wooed by the strength of their attraction and by the sheer luxury of simply indulging in one another. But even so, back then she'd known it couldn't last. Nothing ever did in her life. His life was so totally at the extreme opposite of the scale to hers, and clearly no one had ever said no to him before. At least no one had ever said no and meant it.

"Can I offer you a drink?" Blair said, as Draco stood just inside the door taking in their surroundings.

She supposed that to his eyes it would all look very temporary and not a little bit shabby. For the amount of time she spent here, it did the job.

"No. I didn't come to have a drink with you."

"Then what did you come here for?"

The look in his eyes nailed her feet to the floor where she stood. Heat suffused her body in a slow wave. He wanted her, period. And weakling that she was, she wanted him too.

"Come back to my apartment." His voice was low, slightly uneven. "Come and stay with me until I have to go home."

"I can't."

"Why not? My building's security would give you some peace from these wretched reporters. Besides, you know you want to. Just look at you. Already I can see you're aroused in the way your eyes gleam, in the way you're breathing. If I touched you, your skin would be hot beneath my fingers, and if I cupped your breast I'd feel your heartbeat against my palm."

Breath shuddered from Blair's lungs. She could almost sense his hand against her, so evocative was his tone.

"Come back to my apartment," he coaxed.

"How long?" Blair dragged the edges of her sanity around her like a deflective cloak. Somehow, she had to find the courage to resist him. If she didn't, she knew there could only be heartbreak in store.

"Two weeks, perhaps three."

The thought of continuing where they'd left off the other night rippled through her body in a cascade of longing. Draco had insinuated himself under her skin, into her very psyche. But it wouldn't be forever, she told herself. They had a finite time. They could be together and then he'd leave to reassume his life and she could go on with hers.

She looked around the apartment. Very little of her own personality resided here. Aside from packing some clothes to bring with her, there wasn't anything she'd miss. And yet, if she agreed to this temporary affair— because that's exactly what it would be—could she be certain she'd escape with her heart intact?

"Blair?"

"Yes."

He smiled and her stomach did a little flip-flop in excitement as she absorbed his pleasure in her decision.

"Let me get a few things together, it'll only take me a moment."

Her hands shook ever so slightly as she shoved clothing, underwear and toiletries into a small case. She was mad. Totally and utterly mad to be doing this. But didn't she deserve to reach out and grab some happiness too, however short-lived?

Five

The next couple of weeks saw Blair take her creativity to new heights. After their nights of lovemaking, she expected to leave work each night drained. But instead, the opposite was true. She'd never been more invigorated in her life. She still suffered from the occasional recurrence of nausea or dizzy spell, no doubt still a hangover from the niggling stomach upset she'd had a few weeks ago, but overall she'd never felt better.

Tonight the restaurant was humming, as it had for a while now. This week in particular had been crazy when Draco's friendship with newly-engaged billionaire entrepreneur Brent Colby had been at the forefront of the gossip magazines. It seemed as if every aspect of Draco's life was fodder for the papers, and by association, hers too.

Reporters still hung around outside each night, but instead of the headlines reading things like "Is Carson's Going Italian?" or "Italian Stallion on the Menu?" they were more focused on the increasing high number of local celebrities who'd taken to wanting to be seen at what was rapidly becoming *the* place to be seen.

Blair turned to check the latest round of orders from her wait staff, only to feel the kitchen floor tilt beneath her. *Whoa,* she thought, gripping the stainless steel countertop to steady herself.

"You okay, sweetie?" Gustav hesitated in front of her, his hands and arms filled with entree plates heading out to a group of actors from New Zealand's longest-running soap opera who were celebrating local television award nominations.

Blair swallowed back against the bitter bile that had risen in her throat as the dizziness had hit, and took a steadying breath.

"I'll be fine. You'd better get those out." She gestured to the plates on his arm. "Can't keep the punters waiting, right?"

"Maybe you should get checked out. Who knows, you might have brought back something more than just a gorgeous Italian stud muffin from Tuscany."

Gustav gave her one of his trademark cheeky smiles, but underlying his humor, she could sense he was worried about her.

Blair reached for the bottled water she always kept on hand, and took a long draw from it. That spell had been worse than most, she acknowledged. Maybe she really did need to see a doctor just to get to the root of what ailed her. It wasn't as if it was debilitating, but dizzy spells in a working kitchen were risky at the best of times. And these *were* the best of times, she smiled to herself.

Business had never been better, and at the end of each evening Draco was waiting for her to take her back to his apartment where they'd enjoy a late supper together before retiring to bed. Although there wasn't much retiring in that department.

The next afternoon, when Blair arrived at the restaurant her staff were abuzz with the news that the food critic from *Fine Dining* magazine was reported to be coming to the restaurant that night amongst a bevy of his friends. Blair's nerves shot off the Richter scale as she realized what this could mean.

Tonight could be the night that would realize her dream—or seal her fate into the "almost-ran" category forever. It was imperative that everything be perfect.

She checked and rechecked the storeroom and walk-in-fridge, ensuring that everything she'd ordered was of the highest quality and at its peak of freshness.

Draco let himself in through the back door of the restaurant and waved a quick hello to Blair's sous chef, Phil, who was busy overseeing the kitchen hands' preparations for the menu that night. He was surprised not to see Blair in the kitchen, but caught a glimpse of her in the little office off to the side.

He crossed the distance between them on silent feet. Her back was to the door and she was intent on the computer screen in front of her. The online version of *Fine Dining* magazine, he noted.

He dropped his hands on her shoulders and stroked them down her arms as he leaned forward to kiss her lightly on the back of her neck.

"Draco! This is a surprise," she said with a jubilant smile as she spun round in her computer chair at his touch.

She reached up and pulled his face down to hers. His pulse quickened as her lips pressed against his, then parted, allowing him access to taste her. *Dio,* it seemed as if he could never get enough of her. It would make the news he had to tell her now even more difficult to impart.

"So," she said when he finally drew back from her welcoming embrace, "what brings you here at this time of day?"

"Not so good news, I'm afraid."

"Oh?"

She made a tiny moue with her mouth, making him want to kiss her again.

"I have to go away for a few days, to Adelaide. My Australian business manager has unfortunately been in an accident and won't be out of the hospital for several days. I need to meet with some of our exporters." A sudden thought occurred to him. "Come with me. Leave the restaurant in Phil's hands and run away for a few days. It's beautiful in the Adelaide hills this time of year. You'll love it."

"When do you leave?"

"In a couple of hours. I'm traveling by charter, I'll call them and delay the flight to give you time to get ready. All you have to do is say yes."

Suddenly he wanted her to come with him more than ever. It would be a slice out of time for them both. Granted, he'd have some business meetings and dinners to attend, but he could complete the social side of his business with Blair on his arm. A warm glow started in the pit of his belly as he started to look forward to doing just that. It would be good to get her away from Carson's. She worked as if one possessed her, and he wanted a chance to again see the woman who'd so enticed him while she was at Palazzo Sandrelli.

He studied her face, expecting to see it light up with excitement. Instead a frown pulled her eyebrows together.

"Draco, I'd love to, but I can't. I have a business to run, and tonight—well, tonight is probably going to be the most important night of all."

"Why tonight?" He asked, clamping down on the frustration at having his newly formed plans summarily discarded.

"It sounds as if Bill Alberts—you know, from *Fine Dining*?—will be coming tonight. It's my chance to lift our rating in the magazine. To be the best!"

She glowed with an inner light as she spoke, but for the life of him he couldn't understand why that meant she couldn't come with him. Surely she trusted her kitchen and waitstaff to provide the same level of service they'd give, whether she was there or not.

"So this Bill Alberts, has he made a booking?"

"Not exactly, but one of his associates has made a booking for six guests tonight. It's the way he operates. I just know tonight is going to be *the* night. I have to be here. It's important to me."

While Blair was no further away from him physically than before, he could sense she'd emotionally widened the distance between them.

She pushed her chair back a little, letting it bump against the desk, and stood up. "When do you expect to be back?"

"I'll be gone for five nights." He stepped closer, cupping his hands on her hips and pulling her into him. "Will you miss me?"

He felt the fine tremor run through her before she answered.

"You know I will. But it's okay." She laughed, the sound almost artificial. "It's not as if we have a permanent arrangement together or anything. Now, if you'll excuse me, I have a big night to prepare for."

She went to pull free from his hands, but rather than let her go he tightened his grip, cradling her between his hips. He ran his hands up the long muscles of her back until their bodies were aligned. Her breasts pressed against his chest, full, firm. Different, yet the same. A different bra, perhaps? He couldn't wait to see it, to peel it off her. But in the meantime, he'd have to settle for a kiss that could last him the five nights he'd be away.

He took her lips hungrily, determined to imprint himself indelibly on her both physically and mentally. It bothered him more than he cared to admit that she was prepared to put her work before him, but he reminded himself, it was her intensity, her focus and her drive that he'd found so compelling. The first time he'd seen her, in the kitchens of the commercial arm of the palazzo that catered to groups on culinary tours, she'd stood out from the rest. A humming, vibrant energy amongst a collection of people who only played at being artists in the kitchen.

Blood pooled in his groin and he ground his hips against her, letting his tongue slide into her mouth in a pale imitation of what he wanted to do with her body. She melted against him, her body no longer stiff and reluctant in his arms, but pliant and willing.

The sound of a throat clearing dragged his attention back to where they were.

"You guys want to get a room or something?" Gustav asked from behind him.

"We were just saying *arrivederci.*"

Draco reluctantly let Blair from his arms. The instant feeling of emptiness came as a surprise, but then again, they'd been all but making love here in this tiny cluttered room. It was no wonder that he physically missed her already.

"Gustav, you're here early," Blair said, a warm blush rising up her neck and invading her cheeks.

"Didn't want to miss the show," her headwaiter replied. "The one tonight, I mean—Bill Alberts."

"You people have no proof this man is even coming tonight. Why are you all so...so?" Words failed Draco and he gestured widely with his hands.

Blair caught his hands in hers. "Because this is everything we have worked for for months. If he doesn't show, we'll have had a great trial run."

"But isn't every night a trial run?"

"Of course. But this one could be it. It's as close as

we've gotten. Now, I'm sure you have things to do before you leave tonight, and I know I have a lot to see to."

Draco couldn't believe she was dismissing him! Usually, he was the one to make an exit. He didn't know whether to be annoyed or amused. He settled for amused. He didn't want their parting, however brief this time, to be tainted by any sour words between them. But when he came back he planned to absorb all her attention—to the extent that she wouldn't want to be without him again.

"*Ciao, bella.* Until next Wednesday."

"Take care, Draco."

Her attention was already back on her computer screen before he'd even left the room.

"It's a bugger, isn't it?" Gustav said at his side.

"What is?"

"That she's so absorbed in her work."

"A minor problem, *si.* But nothing that can't be dealt with," Draco replied confidently. With any luck she'd miss him as much as he knew he would miss her in the next few days. It would make his suggestion to her when he got back that much easier to implement.

"Well, good luck, buddy. You'll need it. She's married to this place, you know."

"We will see about that."

He would definitely see about that, Draco decided as his driver pulled away from the front of the restaurant.

Blair picked up the phone and dialed her father's number. He deserved to know that tonight could be the night they'd all been waiting for.

"Dad!" She said the second the phone was picked up, not even waiting for his gruff "hello," then gushed with the news that Bill Alberts could be reviewing them that night.

He was understandably excited for her, and apprehensive. As they finished their call he said, "Well, good luck for tonight, honey. I wish I could be there with you. What about your man, will he be there?"

"Dad, Draco's not my man, he's just—" Blair hesitated, unsure and unwilling to peg a title to exactly where Draco fit into her life right now, let alone examine her growing feelings toward him or how difficult it would be to say goodbye when he returned to his homeland.

"A friend?" Her father laughed in her ear. "Be careful, Blair. He doesn't strike me as the kind of man who takes 'friendship' lightly."

"I know," Blair sighed, "but it will be okay. He's away at the moment, and when he gets back? Well, we'll cross that bridge when we get to it."

A few minutes later, when she hung up, she wondered just how tricky that bridge would be to negotiate. He'd been so *Italian* today, expecting her to drop everything and just be there with him at his behest.

She stared at the wall calendar. Five nights he'd be gone. Five whole, lonely nights. She wouldn't bother going to his apartment, even though she had a key. She preferred the familiarity of her flat, if she was going to be alone.

It was time she changed for work, she thought, flicking a glance at the wall clock, when her eyes drifted back again to the wall calendar. Something wasn't quite right, she thought, looking back over the past two months. She was missing the annotation that marked the start of her period. It wasn't a big mark, just something she did to keep track, out of habit. But since her trip to Tuscany, nothing.

She searched her memory, had she had a period and forgotten to mark it up?

A cold chill settled on her shoulders. No. She knew she hadn't had a period since about a week before she'd gone away. But she'd faithfully taken her pill. There was no way she could be pregnant, could she? She counted two weeks forward from her last period and her finger stopped slap bang in the middle of the week she'd spent at Palazzo Sandrelli. The week that should never have happened. She'd forgone the balance of her culinary tour for the pleasure of being with Draco. Besides, she'd learned so much more from his chefs than she'd have picked up elsewhere.

So what had happened? Was her cycle so out of whack because of the travel and how busy she'd been since her return? But she had been, and still was, on the pill.

Her stomach flipped uncomfortably, reminding her of the nausea, the dizzy spells.

No. She couldn't be pregnant.

Six

"So, you're saying that because I didn't take my tablet at the exact same time every day, being the time I would take my tablet here in New Zealand, that I was unprotected?"

Blair fought back tears as she tried to simplify what her doctor had told her. She'd already left a urine sample with the nurse, but if what her doctor said was true, she had a horrible idea she knew exactly what the result of the pregnancy test would be.

"Blair, you are on a very low dose contraceptive. You were aware of that at the beginning, weren't you?"

"Yes. Yes I was."

And she'd had a reminder set in her cell phone to go off at the exact same time every day so she never forgot a tablet. But since her phone hadn't had a global roaming facility she hadn't taken it overseas with her.

Draco had used condoms when she was in Italy, but after a couple of nights, and days, Blair remembered a couple of occasions where their passion had gotten the better of them. He'd gone to great lengths to assure her of his sexual health, and she knew for herself there were no troubles in that regard. But this, this was another kind of trouble altogether.

The doctor's phone trilled on her desk and Blair jumped, her eyes locked on the doctor's face as he answered.

"Yes, yes. Thank you, nurse."

The doctor turned to face her. Blair could read nothing in expression.

"You say your last period was in the second week of February?" the doctor asked.

Blair nodded. At least that's the last time she'd marked it on her wall calendar. She sat rigid in her chair as the doctor referred to a sheet on her desk.

"Hmmm, well, Blair, that would make you about ten weeks pregnant."

At Blair's shocked gasp the doctor's face settled into sympathetic lines. "Blair, I can tell this is a shock. I take it the father isn't on the scene?"

Blair shook her head, not trusting herself to speak. Pregnant? It was her worst nightmare. How could she have failed so horribly? Risked so much—and lost.

Her mind was numb as she endured the physical examination her doctor requested, and as her appointment came to an end she numbly accepted the slip of paper to order her blood tests.

"Everything looks good so far, Blair. We'll book you in for a scan to confirm your dates, et cetera, but from the exam and your last period I think we can safely assume your baby's due date will be around mid-November."

Mid-November. It seemed so far away, and yet so close too. Blair drove herself back home and curled up on her favorite chair, trying to absorb the reality that she was pregnant—*with Draco's child.*

Oh heavens! *Draco.* He'd be back in two days. How on earth would she keep this from him? He was the kind of man for whom family was everything. She'd understood that early on, when she'd first met him. He'd never support her need to keep working and to keep running Carson's. The kind of family values that defined him had no place in her world. Her world was constantly in motion, moving from one challenge to the next in her field. Carson's itself had only been up and running for three years, the last of which being under her sole guidance.

She had so many plans for the restaurant's development, there was no time for a baby. *A baby.* It was too much to even think about right now. Her life had tilted off its axis with just one stupid mistake. She needed to take stock, find her feet again, to pour herself into something familiar. Even though it was one of her days off, she decided to go into the kitchen and work tonight. She couldn't stand to be alone with her thoughts right now.

Blair peeled off the small dressing that had been secured over her vein where the blood sample had been drawn. The last thing she needed when she went downstairs was for someone to ask her why she'd had blood tests. She would deal with her pregnancy, and Draco, when she absolutely had to.

Draco seethed silently as he listened to Blair refusing to see him. Even as tired and jet-lagged as he was, he couldn't wait to see her again, get her into bed. Unfortunately, she didn't appear to feel the same way.

It frustrated him intensely that she could be so flippant about the connection between them. Not even with Marcella had he felt such passion.

"Blair, didn't you miss me?"

"I did. But it's crazy busy here at Carson's right now. We're fully booked for weeks. We even have a waiting list for diners. Can you believe it? To be honest with you, I'm so tired at the end of each night, it's all I can do to get up the stairs and go to bed."

There was a brittle note to her voice he didn't like.

"Are you brushing me off, Blair?"

"Of course not. It's like I told you. I'm really just too busy to see you, and to be honest, Draco, I just don't have the energy to put into seeing you right now."

"So you're saving all your passion for your work?" he asked lightly, even though inside he was a tumbling roil of rage. "Your dedication is admirable, but what about you?"

"I'm fine. I'm happiest when I'm busy like this. It's what I've always wanted for Carson's, and the rumor is that Bill Alberts was very impressed with his visit here. His online review is due out later this week."

Again, there was that almost-false tone to her speech.

"Blair, is there something you're not telling me? You sound different. Please, let me pick you up tonight and take care of you."

His body hardened as he remembered the first time he'd done just that. Could it only have been just over three weeks ago? It felt longer, just as the past five days and nights in Adelaide had felt longer too. He'd missed Blair on every level, and he had planned a reunion that would satisfy all her senses, not to mention tide them both over for when he had to return soon to Italy. It was disappointing that she wasn't as keen to reunite as he was.

"Blair?" he prompted again in response to her silence.

He heard her draw in a deep breath and exhale heavily before she spoke.

"Look, it's probably better this way anyway. The restaurant is taking all of my time right now and then some. Besides, you'll be gone very soon, and we'd have to say good-bye all over again. I think we should cut our ties before things get too messy."

"Messy?" he asked.

"You know, emotional and all that."

So she thought the life, color and passion in their relationship lacked emotion? He bit against the growl that rose in his throat. More than anything, he wanted to refute her words, needed to coax from her the truth she wouldn't admit to herself.

He'd loved and lost before. When Marcella had died he'd known grief, but it had been heavily laced with guilt. Guilt that he hadn't loved her enough or understood her enough to realize that she would go so far as to risk her own life to give him what he wanted. A sharp pain lanced through him at the memory. It hadn't been just one life, but two.

Marcella should never have gotten pregnant, but she'd hidden from him the details of her congenital heart defect that made pregnancy dangerous, and in her second trimester, she'd paid the awful price for loving him. At a time when most women glowed and blossomed, Marcella had become hypertensive and frail. When her beautiful, generous heart had failed, taking her life and that of their unborn child, Draco had sworn to honor her memory and had promised he wouldn't pass on passion if it presented itself. He may not be ready to love but he certainly couldn't deny the chemistry he and Blair shared.

He cleared his throat before speaking. "And are you telling me there is nothing *emotional* in our connection?"

"There can't be. I won't be that kind of person. It takes too much from me and what I want to do."

"Can you deny that since we have been together your work, your creativity, has bloomed into something that people now stand in line to appreciate?"

"You're being ridiculous."

"Is it ridiculous when you shake with pleasure in my arms? Is it ridiculous when we share an incredible bond at that moment I enter your beautiful body?" He pressed as hard as he dared without making her hang up in his ear.

"Draco, please. Stop." Blair's voice shook.

"Stop? Blair, that sounds suspiciously like emotion in your voice. Without emotion, *cara mia,* we don't really live. Believe me, I know."

"As do I, and I know what I don't want. I'm sorry, Draco. This really has to be good-bye."

The soft click in his ear severed their connection, and for an instant Draco felt that break through his body. He gripped the phone so tight in his hand the plastic squeaked in protest. Slowly, deliberately, he replaced the handset of his phone on its cradle.

Well, as his old professor was always fond of saying, there was more than one way to skin a cat.

Blair made her way out of the lobby of the post office where she'd just picked up her mail. Absently, she flicked through the envelopes as she walked back to her car. Bills, bills—there'd been a time when that fact would have worried her, but not now. The daily receipts were through the roof and the much-coveted and long-awaited five-star review had been posted on the *Fine Dining* Web site. Life had never been better.

Except for the issue of her pregnancy. It had been a week since her confirmation. Five days since she'd severed contact with Draco. She was still in turmoil about whether she should tell him or not. Her favorite option right now was *not,* even if it was horribly wrong. He deserved to know, but she didn't want to tell him. She had no doubt he'd want to take control of her life at that point, and that was not going to happen. Not now, when she had everything else running exactly as she'd imagined when she took Carson's over from her dad.

Blair stopped in her tracks as she came across a high-quality envelope that had been hand-addressed to her. She flipped it over to see who the sender was and frowned as she identified the name as her landlord's lawyers. She'd dealt with them over the lease for

Carson's when her name had been substituted for her father's as the lessee. What on earth could they want from her now?

She unlocked her car and sat down, dropping all the suppliers' invoices on the passenger seat before hooking her finger under the seal and ripping the envelope open. Her eyes scanned the contents of the letter once quickly; then again as she read more slowly, the words sinking in with mind-numbing dread.

The lawyers had been instructed by the owners of the converted villa which housed Carson's that the property had been listed for sale.

She bashed the palm of her hand against her steering wheel in frustration.

"Damn, damn, damn!" she shouted, garnering some strange looks from passersby.

What if a new owner wanted to use the building for something else? They weren't bound by the lease she had with the current owner, an elderly widow. She scanned the letter again for any indication of who might have listed the property, but there was nothing. She'd have to call the lawyers and ask them. She had to find out how much her landlord wanted for the building. Maybe, just maybe, on the coattails of her current success and with the money she'd managed to save, she'd be able to raise a loan to buy the building herself?

The next day, despite not having been able to get ahold of the lawyer dealing with her landlord's affairs, Blair walked as confidently as she could manage into her bank manager's office. She laid out her position and showed him the financial statements for the business, supplemented by her past month's receipts. After much discussion and juggling of numbers, the bank manager leaned back in his chair and steepled his fingers together. Blair's stomach clenched in a knot of nerves.

"Well, Ms. Carson, I think we'll be able to help you out."

He named a figure that made Blair's heart swell with hope, even as her brain shrank back in horror at the requirements to meet such a loan. She couldn't even begin to think how she'd meet the repayments if she had to slow down her workload later in her pregnancy, or how she'd cope after the baby was born.

"Now, I suggest you put an offer together to your landlord's lawyer based on what we've discussed today." He stood up and offered his hand across the table. "Good luck. I look forward to hearing from you so we can get the paperwork drawn up."

"Thank you so much. You have no idea how much this means to me."

"Oh, you'd be surprised. Now you go and make that offer and call me when you hear back, okay?"

"Yes. Yes I will."

Blair almost ran back to her car, barely able to suppress her excitement. The trip back to her apartment passed in a blur. She raced up her back stairs and flung open the door, scrabbling for her phone on the side table before the door was even fully closed behind her.

She drummed her fingers on the tabletop as she was put on hold, the piped music setting her teeth on edge. She was almost on the verge of hanging up to call back and leave a message when the phone was answered at the other end.

Blair wasted no time in getting to the point.

"It's Blair Carson here, I received a letter from you regarding the possible sale of the building I lease from Mrs. Whitcomb. I'd like to put in an offer based on pre-arranged finance."

Blair named the sum she and the bank manager had agreed she could afford. He'd suggested she offer lower and then come back with another figure if the vendor counter-offered, but Blair just wanted the place so much she went in with her highest bid. She curled the cord of the phone around and around in her fingers as she waited for the lawyer on the other side to respond.

"I'm sorry, Ms. Carson. But Mrs. Whitcomb has already accepted an unconditional offer."

"I beg your pardon? But I only got your letter yesterday."

"Yes, the letter was a formality required under your tenancy agreement, however at the time of writing it, the property had already been sold."

"But—"

"As I said, Ms. Carson, I'm terribly sorry. Mrs. Whitcomb was more than happy with the offer and has signed the transfer papers."

"Who…who bought the property?" Tears spiked in Blair's eyes—hot, burning tears of anger and frustration.

"I am not at liberty to disclose the identity of the purchaser at this time."

"And their plans for the building? Have they said anything about that yet?"

"Not yet, Ms. Carson, but might I suggest, as a precaution of course, that you consider where you might relocate to, should the necessity arise."

Blair hung up the phone without saying good-bye and sank to her knees. The tears were coming thick and fast now. *Relocate?* How the heck would she do that? Suitable property in Ponsonby was in very high demand, and with her patronage now at an all-time high, to shift to another suburb could spell total ruin for Carson's.

Raw sobs tore from her throat as she allowed the devastation of the lawyer's words to take full effect. What the hell was she going to do now? Not even when Rhys and Alicia had betrayed her had she felt this distraught, this dispossessed.

It was late afternoon by the time she managed to pull herself together. Downstairs she could hear the noises of preparation in the kitchen. It would be another busy night and she needed to pull herself together and get down there.

Blair dragged herself through a quick shower and put on her double-breasted chef jacket and checkered trousers before lacing up her shoes.

A sense of inevitability settled on her shoulders. What would be would be. She'd find some way to get around whatever the new owner wanted. Besides, why automatically assume that they wouldn't want to keep her on? Carson's made an excellent tenant. Feeling slightly buoyed by the thought, she made her way downstairs.

Gustav bailed her up the minute he saw her.

"What's up, sweetie? You look like you've been through the wringer. Is it your Italian? Do I need to deal with him?"

"No…no, it's not Draco. We've stopped seeing one another anyway. It's—"

Blair's chin started to wobble and Gustav led her straight into her office, pushing her gently down on her chair. He squatted down in front of her and took both her hands in his.

"C'mon, sweetie, let it out. Tell me what's wrong."

"The building's been sold. I tried to buy it but they said it had already been sold."

"But they can't do that," Gustav protested. "Don't you have to be given notice?"

"I got that yesterday, but I thought I'd have time to put an offer forward, that as the tenant I might stand a better chance to buy the property. But it was too late."

"And what about your lease?"

"It's with the previous owner only."

"So it's simple. We renegotiate with the new owner, yes? No need for tears. They'd be mad to lose us here."

"But what if they wanted the building for something else? What if—"

"It'll be okay, just you wait and see. Now dry your eyes and get back into that kitchen. We've got an amazing night ahead."

"Hey, who's the boss here?"

"I am," Gustav answered with a cheeky smile. "I just let you think you are most of the time." He went to leave her office.

"Gus?" she called, making him stop and turn around. "Thanks. I'll see if we can set up a meeting with the new owners and negotiate a new lease in the next few days."

"That's my girl," Gus said with a wink.

The night was chaotic but satisfying. By the time Blair laid her head on her pillow she was too exhausted to even think, let alone dream up possible scenarios for Carson's.

The morning dawned bright and clear—one of those incredibly crisp autumn days that made the sky so blue you felt as if you could stare into its ceiling forever.

Blair contacted the lawyer again and requested a meeting as soon as possible with the new owners. The lawyer said he'd need some time to sort it all out, but when he rang back just before she went into the kitchen, he sounded just as surprised as she did that the new owner had agreed to meet with her the next morning.

She could barely keep her mind on her work, she was so apprehensive about the meeting. But she tried to channel Gustav's positivity, as if by hoping for a positive outcome, it could genuinely make it happen.

The night seemed endless, even after she'd done her final rounds and locked everything up—even after she'd showered and lay in bed for hours, staring at the dark painted ceiling above her.

Finally it was morning. She dressed with extra care, wanting to present the most professional impression of herself and the restaurant that she could.

They'd agreed to meet in the dining room itself at ten, and Blair was pacing back and forth between the tables, wondering for the umpteenth time whether she should have changed from her only suit—a severely cut black number with which she'd teamed sheer black stockings and low-heeled shoes, eschewing a blouse underneath for a wisteria-blue silk camisole she'd treated herself to in Italy—into something less dramatic. The waistband on her skirt was snug, the first visible indication of her pregnancy. She rested her palm against her lower belly. Her baby—Draco's baby—was growing. She wouldn't be able to ignore it for much longer.

The rap at the door made her jump and she wheeled about, taking a second to smooth her hands down over her jacket, giving it a little tug to straighten the edges, before moving across the floor to welcome her new landlord.

"You?" she gasped as she pulled the door open.

A chill ran through her body and the blood drained from her face and dropped to her feet. Draco's frame filled the doorway, his face as dark as thunder, his brows a thick, straight line, and his lips—normally bearing the slight curve of smile—were set in lines that didn't bode well for Carson's, or for Blair.

Seven

"Who else? I couldn't get you to agree to see me any other way. I'm not above using my wealth and influence when I have to. You'd do well to remember that in future, *cara mia*."

"Don't. Don't call me that. I'm not your darling, your lover. Your *anything*."

Suddenly it occurred to Blair that antagonizing Draco was probably not the best thing to have done under the circumstances. A roiling wave of nausea rose from the pit of her stomach. She spun around and flew toward the women's restroom, her hand over her mouth, tears once more streaming down her face.

In a toilet stall she fell to her knees and retched until her stomach was empty.

"Here."

A folded wet paper towel was pressed into her hand from behind her. *Oh no.* Had Draco followed her in here? Witnessed her embarrassing loss of control?

"When you're feeling okay I will be waiting for you outside."

There was a tone to his voice that left her in no doubt that he wouldn't wait long. She freshened up as quickly as she could, rinsing out her mouth before she straightened her jacket again and checked her appearance in the mirror.

Her pantyhose were laddered from the knees down. Well, there was nothing she could do about that right this minute, aside from remove them altogether, and she didn't think he'd wait while she did that. There was one thing about Draco of which she was certain: when he wanted something, or someone, he wanted them right now.

On legs that were surprisingly steady she walked back out to the restaurant. Draco leaned up against the bar, his casually elegant pose a front for the coiled tension she sensed simmering below the surface. He pushed himself upright as she approached and crossed his arms, his feet planted about shoulder width apart.

His dark hair was slicked back off his forehead today, creating a stark demarcation line, framing his face which was set in stern lines. His heavy brows drew together slightly, his green eyes narrowed as his gaze swept her body. She feared he saw everything—each of the changes in her body she'd so staunchly tried to ignore. Her stomach pitched again.

"How long were you going to wait before telling me?" he demanded, his voice like velvet over steel.

She decided to try and bluff him out, then abruptly

changed tack, choosing to attack him on his own terms. "I could ask you the same thing. How long were you going to wait before telling me you'd bought this building? Just how much did you offer Mrs. Whitcomb? I never stood a chance to buy out, did I?"

"You would have known in good time, Blair. Now, it is not like you to be unwell, and I assume it can be due to only one thing. So, I will ask you again. How long were you going to wait before telling me?"

He covered the short distance between them in the blink of an eye. One arm curved around her back, holding her captive against his body. Darn it! Her body responded instantly to his touch, his warmth. When his hand stroked inside the lapel of her jacket and across the silk of her camisole, her nipples tightened instantly, as if seeking the softness of his palm.

"Did you think I would not notice your breasts are fuller?" His hand slid down to her waist before coming to rest against her lower belly. "That your waist is even now thickening with the growth of my child?"

A shiver ran through her from head to foot. There was a note now to his voice that frightened her. A staunch sound of possession, ownership.

"This changes everything. I was prepared to let you have some space, to give you time to see the sense in our relationship. But no more. Not when this involves my child."

"And what about me? You make it sound as if my wishes have nothing to do with whatever you decide."

Draco's lips compressed in a straight line as he looked at her closely. His eyes turned the color of a storm-tossed sea and she shivered again, only this time it wasn't in fear. This time, it was in pure reaction to the intensity she saw there, and every ounce of that intensity was focused on her.

A weaker woman would crumble. Throw herself on his mercy. But then again, she reminded herself tersely, a weaker woman would probably happily accept Draco's imperious manner.

"Well?" she prompted. "Don't I have any say?"

"The baby is a Sandrelli, and he, or she, will be brought up with all that entails," Draco replied in a voice that brooked no argument.

"What are you talking about?" Blair pulled free from his hold.

"I have a responsibility to my family, to the generations of Sandrellis who have gone before me. This baby, this child of ours, has a birthright, a heritage, that stretches back centuries. It will be born where I was born, where my father was born before me and his before him."

Draco struggled to control the rising sense of sheer joy that plumed like a massive cloud of excitement from deep inside him. A baby. A child. *His* child. Finally he could bring his parents something to look forward to, some happiness in lives that had seen altogether too much sorrow. First the death of Lorenzo, his brother, ten years ago, and then more recently, Marcella and their unborn infant and his father's ill health.

No matter what Blair thought, this baby would be born right where it belonged. In the heart of Tuscany.

"You're being unreasonable," she argued. "This is exactly why I would never have told you that I was pregnant. You don't even know yet if it is your baby, and you're already riding roughshod over me and making decisions about it without any thought to how this affects me."

Draco stiffened. "You have been intimate with other men since we met?"

She couldn't hold his gaze, instead letting her eyelids flutter down over her eyes, hiding from him her deepest thoughts. It was all the answer he needed. She could no more deny the baby was his than she could stop him in what he was going to do now.

"You will appoint a new chef to take over from you immediately," he said firmly.

"I will do no such thing. Carson's is my restaurant. I'm in charge here, not you. Besides, I *am* Carson's, as was *my* father before *me!*"

She all but spat the words at him and he fought to control a smile. As if her claim to familial lineage could be compared with the generations-old traditions and responsibilities handed down through his.

"You cannot argue with me on this, Blair. It will serve no purpose."

"No purpose? How dare you. You cannot dictate to me where I live. I have a business to run here, my home is in New Zealand and my baby will be born here."

"If you want to play hardball with me, that is fine. I can match you any day of the week. If you do not agree to return to Tuscany with me and have our baby there, where it belongs, I will terminate your lease on the restaurant. The choice is yours. I will be back this time tomorrow for your answer."

He strode out the door, barely trusting himself to remain in her presence. He'd already lost one child. He would not lose another in this lifetime if he had any say in the matter.

His mind was already ticking over as his driver shot out the car to open the passenger door for him. As he settled against the buttery-soft leather of the interior of the limousine he took his mobile phone from his breast pocket and flipped it open.

His instructions to his New Zealand–based assistant were terse and to the point. "Get me the address of Blair Carson's father. I need it immediately."

Before ten minutes had passed his driver had pointed the limousine down the Southern Motorway and they were headed for an appointment he had no intention of leaving until he had exactly the answer he wanted.

Blair Carson, Sr., was not as Draco had expected. The house in which he lived could barely be called more than a casual beachfront holiday retreat. If his information was correct, the man rented on a month-by-month basis. Hardly the kind of stability that Draco took for granted in his world, and hardly the kind of family stability Draco wanted for his unborn child either.

Draco instantly noted the similarities between the elder Carson and his daughter. Similar height and build, although the man walking toward him now was slightly stooped, his black hair streaked with grey.

He extended his hand, wasting no time in getting to introductions and outlining exactly what he wanted from him.

"So you're telling me my daughter is pregnant?" Blair's dad looked incredulous.

"Yes, sir, and it would mean everything to my family if I could take Blair back to my home in Tuscany to have the baby there. But you know how she feels about Carson's. She isn't happy to leave the restaurant in just anyone's hands. I understand you oversaw the kitchen while she was on her tour in February."

"That's right. It was good to be back in charge." Blair's father nodded, a smile wreathing his face.

"Then, could I presume upon you to do the same again for me while she is in Tuscany until the birth of the child? I will certainly make it worth your while." Draco mentioned a figure that was more than competitive. "I would like you to take over as soon as possible, as I have business to attend to back home, and I would like Blair to travel with me. Obviously, I understand that your health makes it impossible for you to do all that Blair has undertaken in recent months, however, I believe I can trust you to appoint someone in the kitchen who would give her the peace of mind she needs to be able to step away."

"You seem to be prepared to go to a great deal of trouble for my daughter, Mr. Sandrelli."

"Draco, please, and believe me when I say I will do everything in my power to protect Blair through this pregnancy. The hours she's been working, the responsibility and pressure she's put upon herself. None of it can be good, long-term, especially as she gets bigger."

An image of Blair, swollen with his child, sprang into his mind and a rush of pride rose within him so strong and so deep it made his heart ache.

"No, I agree. Well, Draco," Blair's father extended his hand, "it looks as if you have yourself a deal."

"Thank you, sir. You have no idea how much this means to me."

"And Blair? I take it she isn't yet aware of your plans, because to be honest, I know exactly how stubborn she can be, and I can't see her agreeing to this in a hurry."

Draco smiled. Her father knew her well. "I will take care of Blair. You can rest assured of that."

At ten the next morning Draco pulled up outside the restaurant. Before he could rap his knuckles against the glass-paneled door it swung sharply open.

"What have you done?"

Blair looked furious.

"I warned you not to underestimate me. Did you think I said those words in jest?"

"How could you go behind my back before I'd even given you an answer?"

Draco stepped past her and waited for her to close the door before responding. "I did what was necessary."

"Necessary? Do I have to remind you this is *my* restaurant?"

"Not at all, nor do I need to remind you that I own the roof over this restaurant, the walls that surround it and the floor beneath it. You want Carson's to continue, then yes, it will. But it will be without you slaving yourself to exhaustion in the kitchen."

"My father isn't well. He can't take over my role here full-time."

"I'm well aware of your father's limitations, Blair. I'm

not inhuman, despite what you think. He has instructions to appoint a new chef in your absence. However, I think it will do him good to have his hand back in, rather than moldering away where he is now."

"Moldering? He's having a well-earned rest."

"Tell me, Blair, does your father really strike you as the kind of man who would be happy to 'rest' for the balance of his years?"

He could see he'd made his point when she ceased pacing back and forth across the floor and her hands, which had been so animated as she spoke, fluttered uselessly to her side.

Draco stepped closer to her and took her chin in one hand, forcing her to meet his eyes.

"Well? Does he?"

He felt her capitulation in the frustrated breath she let out in a rush through her delectable lips.

"No. He doesn't."

"Then we are settled. We leave at the end of next week."

"What? So soon?"

"There is no reason to linger, Blair. Everything will be under control here. Who is more eminently qualified than your own father to make sure of that?"

"Me. I'm more qualified. I'm younger, I'm fitter and this is my restaurant." Blair's voice rose, her tone becoming frantic.

"And you are also pregnant. Pregnant with my heir. That is a responsibility you must put before all others now."

Her brown eyes blazed her frustration and her fury back into his.

"Fine. I'll go back to your precious palazzo with you. I'll have your baby. But know this, I will return home to New Zealand as soon as I can after the birth."

Draco held his breath a moment, his jaw clenched as he bit back the retort that immediately sprang to mind. Instead, when he spoke, he did so with a voice that was level and which showed no indicator of how he felt inside.

"If you return, it will be without the baby."

Blair's response was vehement. "Whatever it takes to be free of you."

Eight

The next few days turned into a whirlwind of activity. Blair barely had the chance to set foot in the restaurant as Draco commandeered her every waking moment, even going so far as to accompany her to her doctor on the Monday morning before they were due to depart.

She felt odd as they entered the doctor's rooms with him at her side, the breadth of his palm nestled warmly against the small of her back. To all intents and purposes, they'd look just like a normal couple coming for a prenatal visit, but Blair knew they could never be anything so simple.

"Really, Draco. It's only two weeks since I last saw the doctor. Everything's fine. I wasn't due to see her again for another two weeks."

"Let me be the judge of what is fine and what is not," he responded grimly.

Blair rolled her eyes. "Are you a doctor now too?"

"No, I am about to become a father, and I have a responsibility to ensure that my son or daughter is well."

"Honestly, you're overreacting. I'm only twelve weeks pregnant, I've been keeping excellent health, aside from a little tiredness, which," she held up a hand as he started to speak "is perfectly normal at this stage of a healthy pregnancy."

"Ms. Carson? The doctor will see you now," the receptionist summoned them, bringing to a halt any further discussion between her and Draco.

The instant Draco sat down in the doctor's office Blair felt as if she was invisible, as he launched into a series of questions about both her health and the baby's.

"So you can assure me that there are no underlying concerns about Blair's health that could put her or the child at risk?" he asked.

"Certainly nothing we've come across, Mr. Sandrelli. Blair's most recent physical showed her to be in excellent health, with blood pressure, cholesterol, blood sugars—basically everything—within normal ranges. There's no cause for concern that this pregnancy will be anything but smooth sailing."

Blair seriously doubted her blood pressure was within normal ranges at present. Draco's interest in her physical condition bordered on obsessional. Not a side of him she'd ever seen before, and she didn't feel comfortable with it. It was almost as if he'd reduced her to an object, rather than a woman.

"See, I told you everything is fine."

Draco shot a look so bleak that it made her heart

skitter in her chest. "Forgive me my concern, *cara mia,* but I wish to be certain that you and our baby will be safe through this pregnancy."

Blair bristled at his obvious use of endearment to keep the doctor on his side.

"Commendable, Mr. Sandrelli, but let me assure you that I expect no complications for Blair, and I'm sure that while you're back home in Italy you will be able to arrange excellent care for her. In the meantime, here is some literature that may give you some idea of what Blair should be eating, and avoiding—I always think it's kinder on our mothers-to-be if the whole family avoid the foods she has to. Blair is already on folate, calcium and iron supplements, and she has all this information, so I'm sure you can trust her to look after herself equally as well as you." The doctor gave Blair a reassuring smile, clearly well used to dealing with anxious first-time fathers.

"Thank you, doctor. I am much assured."

"Good. Now I'm sure Blair is becoming quite uncomfortable waiting for her scan, so let's take her through to our radiology rooms."

Blair could have hugged the doctor. Let Draco try and sit still with a straining bladder while someone asked inane questions. As they walked through to the radiology rooms, which formed part of the medical center, the doctor continued to talk to Draco.

"I'll receive the scan report and can either have a copy ready for you before you leave for Italy or, alternatively, I can forward a copy to your doctor over there, once you have chosen someone."

"We'd like to take it with us," Draco said before Blair could utter a word. He flipped out a business card. "Please send it through to this address. We leave at the end of the week, I trust that will provide you with sufficient time to get the report to me?"

"Yes, definitely."

The doctor introduced Blair and Draco to the radiographer conducting the scan. Draco sat to one side, now uncharacteristically silent as the radiographer prepared her for the scan by squeezing some gel onto her stomach. The woman described each step in the process of what she was doing as she did it, for which Blair was grateful. This was terrifying territory. Only two weeks ago she hadn't even considered pregnancy, in fact, had purposely avoided any thought of the possibility, now it was very much a reality. Even more so as the grainy image appeared on the screen.

"Here we are," the radiographer said with a smile. "It's time to meet your baby."

Blair's eyes fixed on the screen as the radiographer pointed out the baby's—*her* baby's—legs and arms and its head and body. It was hard to believe this tiny human being was growing and moving within her body, when externally, there was little sign of its existence.

"Oh boy, it's busy, isn't—" Blair turned her head to Draco but never got to finish her sentence as she was suddenly struck by the look on his face.

There was wonder there in his eyes, but at the same time an expression of raw grief that took her breath away. Their current animosity temporarily forgotten, she reached out her hand to him, needing to connect with him, to rid him of the anguish he'd exposed.

At her touch his expression changed and he turned his face, his eyes locking with hers. She was shocked to identify tears in his eyes, and suddenly the reality of the baby and what it meant to him began to hit home.

Already he loved this baby. Already it was a part of him. Yet for her, the pregnancy still felt so foreign. Even the visual evidence on the screen beside her didn't seem real.

The sense of division and separation between herself and Draco yawned like a chasm between them. As if he sensed her thoughts, he gently squeezed her fingers then let her hand go.

"May I have a print-out of the screen?" he asked, his voice surprising Blair with how level it was.

"Sure you can, here I'll print you one each."

Blair wanted nothing more than to curl herself up into a ball in the darkest corner of her bedroom and weep. But even that was lost to her, since her father had moved back into the tiny accommodation in preparation for taking over the management of the restaurant. Now she was back in Draco's apartment, and if the sense of dispossession she felt was any indicator, going to the palazzo in a few days' time was going to be even worse.

Draco settled back into the deep, comfortable leather seat of the charter jet that was taking them home. The week had been a blur of activity, tying off any loose ends to do with his business both in New Zealand and across the Tasman in Australia. He'd barely spent any time with Blair, although he doubted she minded that much at all.

All week he hadn't been able to stop thinking about

the sonogram he kept in his pocket. He'd never attended any of Marcella's checkups with her, he'd always been too busy with work, and she'd understood that—never demanding his company. Now he began to realize all he'd missed out on. It didn't alter the measure of his grief for her or their baby, but he silently vowed he would not be so distant this time.

By the time they reached the private airfield on the outskirts of the Sandrelli land near San Gimignano, they were both weary of travel. The stopovers en route had done little to break the tension between them, and despite the fact that Blair had rested in the private sleeping quarters for several hours, he could tell she was near to dropping with exhaustion. He made a mental note to ensure the obstetrician he'd engaged for her and the baby's care would come to the palazzo.

He wondered how she would find things there now. It would be totally different for her. A temporary home instead of a holiday venue.

The customs officers who met them at the airfield were polite and efficient, welcoming Draco back to his homeland in voluble Italian. Inch by inch, he began to feel his body ease into the rhythms of his land, into the undeniable sense of rightness and belonging he experienced every time he came home. His heart swelled with the thought that, in time, his child would know this feeling too. Would embrace the wide world with all its glories, but would eternally want to return to its roots.

It had been just over six weeks since he'd left, and the land had awakened from the lingering chill of winter that had extended into March. Around them, fields were ablaze with the fire of poppies and the golden glow of wild mustard.

Yes, it was good to be back.

Once the official requirements had been met, Draco ushered Blair into the waiting limousine. As they neared the palazzo, Draco looked around him with great eagerness, observing the various plantings that sustained part of the business enterprises of the Sandrelli Corporation. Olive groves, in the peak of health, marched like a giant green army over the gently rolling hills, while on the rise of land leading up to the palazzo lay row upon row of grape vines. At the top of the hill, inured against marauding invaders by a 16th century stone wall, stood the palazzo. Home.

It was good to return to what were essentially the grass roots of his heritage.

He flicked a glance at Blair. She sat pale and rigid on the seat, her eyes fixed out her window. She had barely said a dozen words on this final leg of the journey. He hoped she would be able to relax, once settled back into the palazzo. For both her sake and the baby's.

Once inside the palazzo, Draco led Blair to her room.

"This is different from where I stayed before, isn't it?" Blair noted as they went up a wide staircase to the next floor.

"Yes, this leads to my private quarters. Where you stayed before was the wing we have reserved for guests, both corporate- and tourism-related."

"I had no idea the accommodation was so extensive here. I really only saw such a small part of it, didn't I?"

Draco nodded, his mouth pulling into a wry smile.

If you counted the commercial kitchen, where the culinary tour classes were given, and her sleeping quarters of the time, the part she saw was indeed small.

"I will give you a full tour of the palazzo when you're rested. Perhaps tomorrow, hmmm?"

"I'd like that."

Was that an overture of friendship? He realized she must feel completely displaced. Not even the room she'd be sleeping in now was familiar to her. He swung open the heavy, paneled door that led into her room. In the warm glow of the evening, the deep rose-pink drapes, edged in gold braid and tied back from the mullioned windows, looked friendly and inviting, as did the canopied 19th century bed that dominated the room.

"Oh my God, it's like a museum. Are you sure I can sleep here?" Blair said with a nervous laugh.

"These pieces have been in my family—well—since they were new. We use them. That's what they were designed for."

Draco gestured to one of his staff to put Blair's cases through another door on one side of the room.

"A maid will be along shortly to unpack for you."

"Oh, that won't be necessary. I can do that for myself." Blair protested.

"It is very necessary. You look shattered. Why don't you turn in early and in the morning we can start anew? What do you say?"

There was something in Draco's eyes that went straight to Blair's heart. *Start anew.* It was so appealing. If only she could start anew back to February when she was last here. Where would they be now? She certainly wouldn't be here. She'd be back at Carson's doing what she loved.

Well, she decided she could make herself miserable for the whole time she was here, or she could make the most of it.

"Thank you, I'd like that," she replied softly.

Draco lifted a hand and traced one finger along the line of her jaw. Instantly her nerve endings went crazy. He hadn't touched her since that brief moment when they'd clasped hands in the radiography room. Suddenly she realized just how much she missed his touch. Missed him. Tears sprang to her eyes. Stupid, helpless tears that did nothing to reflect the jumble of emotions that cascaded through her.

"I'll let you rest then." Draco turned to leave the room.

"Draco, wait. Where will you be?" To her horror a note of panic slipped into her voice.

"I will call in briefly to see my parents and then I will return. I'll be just two doors further down the corridor, in my suite. Do not worry, Blair. I will not let you go far from my sight."

Blair nodded, barely trusting herself to speak.

"*Buona sera,* Blair. Sleep well. And don't worry about the maid when she comes, she will use the door that leads straight to your dressing room, so as not to disturb you."

"D-dressing room? I barely have enough clothes to fit in a chest of drawers, and now I have an entire dressing room?"

"Perhaps we can fly to Livorno, on the coast, for the day, and do some shopping. Or even north to Firenze.

Clearly, you will need a new wardrobe, especially as the baby grows."

The excitement that began to bubble inside her fell immediately flat as she was reminded that the true purpose behind her being here was the baby, and the baby alone.

"As you wish," she managed to say, because all of a sudden it was quite clear to her that despite the exquisite furnishings and the plush elegance of her new temporary home, she was here only at his bidding.

"Blair? It is not just as I wish. I would like to think you're looking forward to this baby too. I know we said some harsh things to one another last week, but I meant what I said when I suggested we start over. Think about it, hmm? And I'll see you in the morning."

When Draco was gone Blair took a minute to familiarize herself with her room. The large en suite bathroom was as luxuriously fitted as the bedroom—although a great deal more modern, she noted with relief. She grabbed her toiletries and a night shirt from her case and prepared for bed.

Draco's parting words still rang in her ears. *Start over.* It would be so lovely to do so. But what of her dreams? She'd finally taken Carson's to five-star splendor, only to have to leave it in another's hands. Granted, that person was her father, but still she felt cheated.

She slid between the fine cotton sheets, laundered with a hint of lavender, and rested her head onto the pillow. She'd thought she had it all under control, but where was that control now? Firmly in Draco's hands, and there was nothing she could do about it. Absolutely nothing.

Nine

Blair was awakened the next morning by the clink of crockery on a tray.

"*Buon giorno,* Ms. Carson. I trust you rested well." A uniformed maid bustled into the room and placed a tray on a nearby table. "I have brought you breakfast and a request from the *Signore* to be ready in an hour for a tour of the property. And Ms. Carson, the coffee is decaffeinated as per your doctor's instructions."

"Thank you," Blair shoved herself upright in the bed and sniffed the air as the aroma of freshly brewed coffee tantalized her nostrils. Her eyes spied pastries in a small basket on the tray. "Are those *cornetti?*"

"Yes, raspberry. Your favorite, *si?* Cristiano, our cook, he remembered, and Ms. Carson? There is a small gift here for you also. A welcome to the palazzo from the *Signore*."

Both curious and ravenous, Blair pushed the bedcovers from her legs and rose from the bed. With a cheerful smile, the maid left the room.

A narrow, long blue-velvet jeweler's box nestled on a starched, white serviette, next to the plate of *cornetti*. Curiosity won the tug of war and she lifted the case and gently opened it. Inside, laid upon shining white satin, was an exquisite silver charm bracelet. Blair lifted it from the case and held it up, exclaiming over the delicate charms evenly spaced along its length.

She didn't usually wear any jewelry. It just got in the way in the kitchen, but for now, she couldn't wait to put this piece on. She struggled a little with the parrot clasp before managing to secure it round her wrist. She turned her arm this way and that, admiring the reflection of light on the silver and the faint jangle of the charms as they bumped together. How thoughtful of Draco to give this to her. But then her cynical, insecure side wondered if he kept a cabinet filled with such things for his female guests. She knew for a fact that he was highly sought after in international circles. Just about every article about them back home in New Zealand had put pictures of his past companions side-by-side with whichever one they'd managed to snap of her and Draco together. Whatever the case, she loved the bracelet and she'd enjoy wearing it.

Her stomach rumbled, reminding her of the sweet delights waiting for her. Blair's mouth watered as she tore off a piece of the fresh pastry and popped it in her mouth. For a moment, even her critical chef's brain disengaged as it melted on her tongue. By the time she'd picked up the last crumb and enjoyed the delicious nutty-flavored coffee, she was ready to face the day. She took a quick shower in the bathroom and dressed in a loose-fitting, raspberry-colored sundress, as the day promised to be warm. The button-down style was easy to wear, and then, just for something different, she grabbed a long, multicolored scarf and tied it across her head from above her fringe and twisted it into a knot at the nape of her neck. The tails dropped over her shoulder. She studied the effect in the mirror. It was kind of retro sixties, but with her coloring, it looked good and gave her a dose of much-needed confidence. She looked at the time. She was ready early.

She paced the floor of her bedroom for a few minutes, finally settling in front of the tall windows that gave a stunning view out across the valley. In the distance, the darker shadows of the hills loomed over the verdant countryside. How different the landscape was from the blanket of winter she'd seen last time she was here. She wondered if she was to wait here for Draco, or if she should see if he was in his room. Waiting didn't sit comfortably with her. Already she was itching to get out in the sunshine of what promised to be a beautiful spring morning. Her decision made, she spun around and opened the door.

He'd said last night he was a couple of doors down the corridor from her. Her shoes made no sound on the petit point carpet of the hallway. It almost felt sacrilegious to walk on the fine craftsmanship. A couple of doors down he'd said; a rueful smile twisted her lips. He neglected to mention just how far down the hallway a couple of doors actually was.

Blair hesitated when she reached the cream-and-gold paneled door, a twin to her own. She drew her fisted hand up and rapped gently on the wood. It opened almost immediately.

"*Buon giorno,* Blair. You look much better this morning."

"Thank you. I had a wonderful sleep. And thank you too for this." She held up her wrist.

"Ah, you're most welcome. Here, come in, I'll be ready in a moment."

Draco stepped aside and Blair walked into a comfortable sitting room. While the chairs were heavily upholstered in rich floral fabrics, there was nothing feminine about the room. The wood-paneled walls and hunting paintings took care of that little detail, Blair noted.

She felt Draco as he drew up behind her. "You look and smell wonderful today."

A small shiver ran through her body as he dipped his head to the curve of her neck and felt his hand run down her arm. His long fingers wrapped around her wrist and he lifted her arm.

"Each charm has a special significance to our land here and our place in it." He fingered the small wine bottle nearest the clasp. "This is for the vineyard, where we produce our own Vernaccia."

"That's the white wine I had when I was here before, isn't it? I tried to get it in for Carson's, but our wine merchant was unable to secure any for me."

"We'll have to see what we can do about that, for your father."

Blair bristled slightly at the assumption that she would not be equally interested in getting the wine to New Zealand, but she was distracted by the soft stroke of Draco's index finger on the pulse point at her wrist.

He continued to hold her wrist loosely as he detailed each of the other charms on the chain, and she found herself mesmerized by the cadence of his voice. When he was finished she realized she'd allowed herself to sink back against his body, his chest a warm imprint through her dress and along her back.

She straightened, pulling loose from his clasp, feeling unsettled that she'd fallen under his spell again so easily. Last night he'd suggested they start over, but now in the light of day, she wasn't so convinced it was such a good idea. He was very much the lord and master of all the land she could see from the windows of the palazzo. So where did that leave her? And where did that leave her responsibility to Carson's?

"Draco, could I use a phone to let Dad know we arrived safely and that I'm okay? I saw one in my room but I wasn't sure if I could use it for an international call."

"No matter, I have already called him. He was happy to hear you were settled and that the journey was behind you. He said when you arrived back in New Zealand in February the trip had taken a lot out of you and that it took you a few days to recover from jet lag. Hopefully, you won't be so affected this time."

"After the luxury of that plane trip? I doubt it."

Blair smiled, hiding the flair of irritation that Draco

had spoken to her father without her knowledge. She'd have liked to have touched base with him, heard how he was managing back in the restaurant without her there.

"You are worrying about your precious restaurant, aren't you?"

Was she so easy to read? "Yes, I am. And about Dad too. When we left he'd done nothing about employing a new chef. I'm concerned he'll push himself too hard."

"Blair, your father is a grown man, quite capable of making his own decisions."

"That's exactly what I'm worried about. It was the decisions that he made that made him ill the last time."

"But he is on medication, *si?*"

"Yes, but he's stubborn." *Like you,* she added silently.

"Why don't you call him tonight around ten? It'll be eight o'clock Sunday morning there."

"Damn, I forgot about the time difference," Blair muttered, remembering it was the time difference that had gotten her into this position in the first place. "What about now? It'll be evening there now, right? About seven?"

"But won't the restaurant be busy? He'll hardly have time to talk to you, and he already knows you are safe and well."

What Draco said made perfect sense. "All right. Tonight it is."

"Good. Now we have that settled, let's start on our tour. Which do you prefer first—the palazzo or the grounds?"

"Oh, the grounds, please. It's such a beautiful day."

"Your wish is my command," Draco responded with a smile that sent a bolt straight to her heart.

He offered her his arm and she rested her hand in the

crook of his elbow. As they made their way back down the corridor toward the stairs, Draco told her of the history of some of the pieces of furniture and ornaments.

"Doesn't it worry you that some of these things will get broken? Shouldn't they be in a museum?"

Draco laughed. "They are a part of my family. If they break, they break. Of course, we take every step to ensure that doesn't happen on a regular basis, and some of the more valuable pieces are locked away in glass-fronted cabinets, like the ones you would have seen in the salon used for tour guests."

Blair envied him his casual acceptance of his world. As welcoming and comfortable as the palazzo was, she doubted she could ever fit in here. Her upbringing had been so transient, she didn't even have school photos to look back on. Whereas Draco—she looked around at the portraits interspersed with deep windows along the corridor—he could trace back his ancestors to near-medieval times.

Draco led her outside the palazzo to a courtyard where a gleaming convertible sat awaiting them.

"We're going to drive?" Blair asked, surprised. She'd expected they'd be walking around the grounds.

"I thought I'd take you to the furthest point of our land and then work our way back. Would you prefer we stay closer to home?"

Home. His home perhaps, Blair thought, looking back at the size of the palazzo as he helped her into the car.

"No, that's fine. It'll be lovely, I'm sure."

Draco slid into the driver's seat, his strong, capable hands settling on the steering wheel. It occurred to Blair that this was the first time she'd seen him drive.

"You don't drive when you're in New Zealand. Why is that?"

"Parking in and around the city is at such a premium, I prefer not to be bothered with such things when I'm there on business. Generally, I keep a car there for my own use, but for pleasure, I prefer to use my motorbike when I'm in Auckland."

"You ride a bike?"

Blair was surprised. Draco had always struck her as so smooth and urbane. Imagining him in black leathers, astride a powerful bike, did strange things to her equilibrium.

"Sure. My friends, Brent and Adam, and I each have the same model Moto Guzzi. When we're all in town together we try to make a few road trips, get away from it all. This time it didn't happen, but there's always the next."

By Brent and Adam, Blair knew he meant multimillionaire entrepreneur Brent Colby and Adam Palmer. Both men featured frequently in the papers, both in the business section and the social reports. And judging by the media storm about Brent Colby and heiress Amira Forsythe, just before she and Draco had left Auckland, that popularity wasn't about to die down terribly soon.

"How did you three meet? You were all at the memorial service, weren't you? Did you go to school at Ashurst?" she asked.

"Yes. My parents felt it was important that both my older brother and I experienced education in another country. He went to Australia, I went to New Zealand."

"Your brother?"

"Yes, Lorenzo. He died ten years ago. A stupid

accident. One of those totally avoidable things. He was waterskiing with friends off the Amalfi Coast. Unfortunately, the driver of the other boat had been drinking and thought it humorous to play 'chicken' with the boat towing Lorenzo. His neck was broken in the impact. He died immediately."

Tears filled Blair's eyes. "Oh, Draco, I'm so sorry. That must have been awful for your family."

He turned to face her, lifting a hand to gently wipe away the tears that spilled over her lashes and down her cheeks.

"It was terrible, but we've learned that life must go on. And now we have a new life to look forward to, our baby. My parents—you have no idea what this will mean to them."

"You haven't told them yet?"

Blair knew Draco's mother and father lived in a more modern home on the Sandrelli land, and she half-expected Draco to introduce her to them today.

"No, when I saw them last night I didn't feel the time was right. My father was tired and my mother distracted by his health. I will let them know soon, though. Now, shall we begin our adventure for today?"

Blair nodded her agreement and he shifted the car into gear, the wheels spitting up a little gravel as they drove out the massive gated entrance to the palazzo grounds.

She was amazed at the diversity of the land here, and the way it was used. As they passed each different business unit she was reminded of the charm bracelet Draco had given her this morning. Each charm truly was representative of the expanse of the Sandrelli family's endeavors. She began to feel a new respect for him and for the responsibility that sat so well on his shoulders.

Draco felt the familiar swell of pride as he showed Blair over the land that was as much a part of him as the blood running in his veins. It was always a pleasure to see the property through another's eyes, but this time it was even more important that Blair fully understand what it meant to be a Sandrelli. What it would mean to their son or daughter.

They were about halfway back toward the palazzo when Draco pulled off the road and drew the car up a private road leading through a massive olive grove.

"Would you like to stop for some lunch?" he asked, and was surprised to catch her stifling a yawn.

"Oh," she laughed, embarrassed, if the flush on her cheeks was anything to go by. "Yes, that would be lovely."

Draco took a right turn down a barely visible lane and drew the car to a halt under the trees.

"Cristiano packed a lunch for us when I told him we'd be out for the day. Just give me a minute and I will have it ready for you."

"Anything I can do to help?" Blair asked, swiveling her long legs out of the car and standing.

She slowly stretched out her back and lifted her arms above her head. Instantly a shock of desire pummeled through him like a bolt of electricity. Even with the new fullness her body now began to display, she sent every particle in his body into overdrive. She went still as she realized he was watching her.

"Is there something wrong?"

"No. Nothing is wrong. You look beautiful today. The setting suits you."

"Flatterer," she said, smiling, then and came across to him, taking the rubber-backed rug from his hands and shaking it out onto the ground in the sunshine.

"It's the truth," Draco replied. "I do not waste my time on lies."

"Yeah," Blair said, softly. "I had noticed that about you."

A tight smile pulled at his lips. *What else had she noticed about him,* he wondered.

He lifted the cooler from the trunk of the convertible and put it beside the rug. Blair was already sitting cross-legged on the blanket and had eagerly lifted the lid off the cooler and started to put the plates of food and containers of drink onto the rug, using the lid as a small table. Draco grabbed the small loaves of fresh bread Cristiano had baked early this morning and dropped down next to her.

They began to eat, Draco making the most of the setting to explain a little about the olive oil process in Tuscany. Blair had missed the harvest, which had taken place late autumn, the cooler valleys in the region demanding the harvest occur earlier than in other parts of the Mediterranean, and she was fascinated by his description. But before long she was yawning once more.

"I'm sorry, Blair, I didn't mean to exhaust you on your first day back here."

"It's not that. I've really enjoyed everything you've shown me today. Perhaps it is just a little jet lag still."

"So sleep."

"Here?" Blair waved her hand.

"Why not? We won't be disturbed. The sun is warm. Lie back and relax."

"I can't," she protested. "I don't sleep during the day. It's just so…"

"Decadent?" he asked, smiling. Yes, he'd bet she never let up during the day. But if she was going to do the best thing by his baby she would learn to slow down. "So be decadent for a change. Lie down and relax."

Blair did as he suggested.

"I bet I won't sleep."

"We will see. Just listen to the land. Let the sun caress your skin. And relax. Simple, really."

He watched as her eyelids fluttered closed and smiled again as he saw the tension in her body, as if she was coiled, ready to spring to the next activity. Eventually though, her breathing began to deepen, the muscles in her body slacken. He gave a small nod as she finally slept.

Draco stretched out beside her, taking care not to touch her, but instead watched her. Lying on her back as she was, it was easier to see the subtle changes the pregnancy had wrought on her body so far. The ever-so-slight fullness of her breasts, the tiny rounding of her lower belly, the new roundness to her cheeks which had always been so angular.

He liked the changes, liked what they did for her. Made her appear less untouchable. And just like that, he ached to touch her. To see her naked. To rediscover the intimacy they had shared. And, by the time Blair woke forty minutes later he knew exactly how their afternoon would progress.

Ten

As her eyes opened and she became aware of their surroundings, he leaned over and slanted his mouth across her. A teasing touch, but one that had the power to immediately wring a tiny moan of want from her. Her eyes darkened even more, until her pupils almost consumed the rich chocolate of her irises. A sigh drew past her lips and he breathed it in.

He bent his head to her again, this time taking his time to make love to her lips with his own, drawing her lower lip between his, sucking gently on the tender skin, stroking along its fullness with his tongue.

A shudder ran through him as Blair traced her tongue against his upper lip, in a mirror of what he was doing to her. He let go of her lip and deepened their kiss, hungry for more of her. He positioned himself over her body, holding himself up and away, but feeling her heat imprint through the layer of his clothing and against his skin.

Blair ran her hands up the cords of his arms and he reveled in her touch, in her enthusiasm as her lips met his again and again, as their tongues dueled and tangled together. This thing between them he could understand. It was as elemental and as vital as the energy of the land beneath them.

He supported his weight on one arm and with his other hand flicked open the top buttons of her dress, following the path of his fingers with his mouth. The fabric fell away, exposing the sheer white lace bra that cupped her breasts…breasts topped with hardened rosy peaks that begged for his caress. He lined the edge of her bra with his tongue, following the scalloped pattern with his utmost attention, then swooped against the tight bud pressing against the fine lace. He covered her nipple, still encased in material, with the heat and wetness of his mouth, and drew her into him.

Blair let out a low-pitched scream, her lower body arching to meet his as he grazed his teeth against the sensitive nub, over and over, before doing the same to its twin. Her hands fisted on his shoulders, squeezing tight. He'd bear the marks of her fingernails, he was certain, and the thought brought a smile to his lips.

Draco continued to unbutton her dress, finally baring her skimpy lace panties to view. He cupped her, pressing his palm against her, discovering her wetness, her heat. She squirmed against him and suddenly he could play with her no longer.

His plan to make slow, leisurely love to her would

have to wait until another time. A time, perhaps, when the very essence of her didn't drive him crazy with need. He ripped his shirt open sending buttons flying, desperate to feel the texture of her skin against his, then lowered his chest to contact hers. But there was still the barrier of her bra. He gently coaxed her up, sliding the straps of her sundress off her shoulders, and with deft fingers reached behind her to unsnap her bra.

Tiny goose bumps raised on her skin as he peeled it away.

"Are you certain you want this?" Draco asked, his voice as coarse as gravel. She could refuse him now, and he'd manage to hold back.

"I want this. I want...*you*."

Her words were his undoing. Blair knotted her fingers in his hair and dragged his face down to hers, and he groaned into her mouth as their skin touched, as her nipples pressed against his skin, as their warmth commingled and combined to ignite into a need for more.

Her hands slid down his back, squeezing and kneading his muscles, as if she couldn't get quite enough of him. Then they were at the waistband of his pants, unbuckling his belt with a dexterity he doubted he was still capable of, and sliding the zipper open, pushing the fabric down over his buttocks.

He flexed against her then. He could no longer hold himself back. To his eternal frustration, they each still bore a layer preventing him from reaching his goal. Draco drew up onto his knees and eased her panties off her. God, she was so beautiful, dappled with sunlight and shadows. A knot built up in his chest. He hesitated a moment longer, drinking in the sheer joy of her glory, then his desire asserted itself once more. Dispensing with his footwear and clothes took but a second.

Blair's legs fell apart as he knelt between them and positioned himself at her entrance.

"Tell me again that you're certain."

"Draco, please. I want this. I want this so much."

"Then I shall give you what you want," he growled.

He reached beneath her buttocks, angling her hips to meet his, then slowly—ever so slowly—allowed his length to penetrate her heat. As he did so, his eyes met hers and held them, the intimacy of their look lending a new poignancy to his possession of her body. Her eyes widened as he slid deeper, still taking his time, until he was buried within her.

Sweat beaded on his upper body as he fought to control the urge to plunder her. But he forced himself to hold back, to make this last as long as humanly possible.

Blair wrapped her legs around his hips, holding him to her, and rocking her pelvis gently against him. He shook with the effort of staying still, of concentrating on the sensation of her movements, of the clench and release of her inner muscles. Over and over, until he was nearly mindless with passion.

His hands gripped her hips and he surged back, before sliding home again. He'd never felt this way with another woman. Never experienced this sense of vulnerability or level of need before in his life. Instinct overtook reason, as he set up a rhythm calculated to drive them both to shattering completion.

His climax ripped through him just as he began to feel her body tighten and bow beneath his, and he gave himself over to the waves of pleasure that pulsed between them. His whole body shook as he lay down beside Blair, pulling her body up and over his so they could remain joined for just that moment longer. She sagged against him, her heart beating furiously against his chest, her breathing as ragged as his own.

This is life, he thought, as he smoothed his hand down her back and cupped her buttocks, pulling her tight against his body, as if they could stay like this forever. *This is living.* Anything else he'd done before today, before this moment, had merely been a rehearsal.

They dozed together in the sunshine, oblivious to all but the slowing of their breath, the even rhythm of their heartbeats, the languorous warmth enveloping them. But even so, a darkness hovered on the periphery of Draco's thoughts. It was Blair's determination to return to New Zealand once the baby was born.

No matter how perfect their physical union, she had no intention of staying, of creating a family with him. He'd had to threaten her precious restaurant before she would agree to come home with him. The reminder was sobering and took an edge off the pleasure that had saturated his senses.

Draco stirred, as uncomfortable now with his thoughts as he was with the hard ground beneath his back. He needed some distance from Blair, time to regroup his thoughts, remind himself what they had was lost.

"Come," he said softly, stroking her short, black hair with a steady hand. "We should think about heading back."

Blair groaned in protest but disentangled her limbs from his and slid off his body in a sensuous glide. She slipped her underwear back on and watched from under her lashes as Draco did the same. Her body hummed with satisfaction but her mind whirled with confusion.

Where did this leave them? Continuing their affair while he'd been staying in Auckland was one thing, but what had happened today changed things again. When Draco practically forced her here she would never have believed that within twenty-four hours of their arrival they'd be making love. And it had been lovemaking. He'd been so reverent, so tender with her. She knew at any time she could have called a halt to his attention, but she hadn't wanted to.

She wanted to make love with him again. The heightened sensitivity of her skin, her breasts—nearly every molecule in her body—had made the entire experience one she ached to repeat.

She dragged her creased sundress back on and found her head scarf, which had slipped off her hair at some stage during their lovemaking. Only when she was fully clothed could she meet Draco's eyes.

He had packed away the cooler and its contents into the back of the car, and now stood, tall and straight and endearingly handsome, looking into the distance. He turned and caught her eye. A small smile briefly twisted his lips, sending a jolt of desire through her again.

Blair scrambled to her feet and thrust them into her

sandals, then picked up the blanket to give it a shake and fold it back up again. Draco took the blanket from her, his fingers lingering a moment as they grazed hers.

"We will have to do this again, before it grows too warm."

"I'd like that," Blair answered, holding eye contact. Trying silently to tell Draco that she'd like that and more.

He'd tucked the tails of his shirt in at the waistband of his black trousers, but the absence of buttons meant closing the edges of the fabric was impossible. Her gaze was drawn to the smooth, golden planes of his chest. Without thinking, her tongue swept her lips.

"If you keep looking at me like that, we may not get home before dark," he said, with a note of humor in his voice.

But beneath the humor there was something else that Blair couldn't quite put her finger on. It was almost as if he'd created some mental distance between them. She felt the distance widen as he opened the car door for her and gestured for her to get in. Once she was seated he closed the door and walked around to his side of the vehicle.

Draco barely spoke on the journey home, and as they re-entered the palazzo he made his apologies, saying he had work to attend to. Blair watched him go.

"Draco?"

He hesitated and turned to face her, his face inscrutable. *"Si?"*

"Is something wrong?"

"Nothing is wrong. I will see you at dinner at eight. If

you need me for anything before then, you'll find my office extension on the list next to the phone in your room."

Blair nodded, but her mind latched on to his expectation that she'd spend the rest of her time in her room. Banished perhaps?

She certainly needed to shower and freshen up, but she'd be darned if she was going to spend the next few hours hemmed up in her room, no matter how beautiful it was. There was plenty she could explore before meeting Draco for dinner.

After Blair had showered and changed, she went back to the ground-floor level of the palazzo and headed in what she hoped would be the direction to the kitchen. If Cristiano was there preparing for their evening meal, she wanted to see if she could lend a hand. And if she couldn't help, maybe she could learn something that she could take back home with her.

Large glass-and-wooden doors led off a gallery and onto a wide, tiled patio, and the shine of late afternoon sun on water distracted her from her intentions to find the kitchen and instead led her outside. Topiaried orange trees and low box hedging defined a beautiful formal garden. A few yards away a large stone building squatted—an old stable by the look of it—its golden brick bathed in sunshine. Blair meandered along the pathways, intrigued by the building ahead.

As she got closer she could see inside the deep, arched windows. State-of-the-art gym equipment took possession of the carpeted floor. Here was something else she could fill her time with, she thought. She wondered if the large outdoor pool, further off to her right, was heated. Between the two, the gymnasium and the pool, at least she could keep her fitness up.

At home, being constantly on the run with the restaurant, she'd never had to worry about her fitness, but now—being virtually on holiday until the birth of the baby—she would have to keep "in shape" or she'd struggle to keep up her pace when she returned to work.

Eventually, Blair began to make her way back toward the palazzo, and with a soft exclamation of delight realized the herb garden she'd come through had led her to her original destination—the palazzo kitchen. A wide door stood open, and beyond it she identified hanging copper pots and a large black coal range.

"Hello?" she called from the door.

"Ms. Carson! It is a pleasure to see you again!"

Cristiano bustled across the terra cotta-tiled floor and clasped Blair exuberantly to his rotund figure.

"Cristiano, lovely to see you too. Please, call me Blair. I was wondering if I could help you with anything for tonight, I'll go mad if I don't have something to do."

The cook made a rude noise and flapped his hands toward the long wooden table that dominated the center of the kitchen.

"Sit down, sit down. You're not here to work. You can watch and learn instead," he answered with a wink.

Blair did as she was told and sank into one of the cane-bottomed wooden chairs at the table. Time passed quickly as Cristiano peppered Blair with questions about what she'd been doing since she left the palazzo back in February. She found it hard to believe that it had been less than three months since she was here, even harder to believe she was back.

She smiled at Cristiano's voluble sighs and laughter, as she told him about Carson's latest achievement and how the restaurant had grown from seventy-percent capacity to over a hundred-percent bookings, weeks in advance. But she itched to throw on an apron and work alongside him.

An idea sprang to mind and before she could think it through further Blair found the words spouting from her mouth.

"Cristiano, if I don't cook while I'm here I think I'll go crazy. Besides which, when I go back home I will need to bring something new again to the restaurant. Could I take some lessons from you? I know you often conduct demonstrations when tours come through to the palazzo. Would it be too much of an imposition if you coached me privately?"

Before the chef could reply, his eyes flew to one of the internal doorways.

"Blair, you aren't here to work."

Blair stood rapidly at the sound of Draco's voice. Small black spots swam before her eyes and she put a hand out to the back of her chair to steady herself a moment. When the spots receded Draco was at her side.

"Are you all right?" he asked.

"I'm fine, just got up a little too quickly, that's all," she brushed aside his concern. "And for what it's worth, I wouldn't think it work to have the chance to learn some new dishes from Cristiano."

Draco shot a glare at Cristiano before the other man

could speak. "We will discuss this later. For now we have other, more important matters to discuss. Can you come with me now or would you like to sit a while?"

"Draco, I'm not an invalid. I told you, I'm okay."

Where had the man who'd been such a tender lover this afternoon disappeared to? she wondered. The Draco she saw now was more like the overpowering man who'd bought her restaurant building out from under her so he could control where she lived and where she bore his child.

He said something in rapid Italian to Cristiano, who answered in kind before turning back to his work.

"Come with me," Draco said, offering Blair his arm.

Irritated by his high-handed attitude, she fell in step beside him, but refused to touch him. He led her to a salon that looked out over the formal garden she'd found near the gymnasium. Ripples of light from the swimming pool reflected through the deep-arched wood-and-glass doorways onto the high ornate ceiling. Blair felt as if, in many ways, she'd stepped into another world. Certainly she was out of her world.

She sat on the edge of a richly upholstered sofa and gestured to the gymnasium across the garden.

"I was thinking I could use the gym, would that be okay?"

"The gym?" He frowned a little.

"Yes, and the pool too, if it's warm enough. If I'm not doing anything else, I'd like to at least have some regular exercise."

"The pool is heated, but we will wait and see what

the doctor has to say first. I have made an appointment for you to see a specialist tomorrow."

"A specialist?" Blair shot to her feet. *How dare he go ahead making appointments without discussing things with her first?* "Whatever for? I'm fit as a horse. I've barely even been sick. Besides, I spent some time checking on the Internet before we left Auckland, and there's an extremely well-appointed birthing center not far from here," she protested.

"A birthing center?"

"Yes, run by midwives. It's a perfectly safe and professional environment for me to have the baby."

"Safe." Draco's jaw tightened, a sign she was rapidly identifying as a precursor to his controlled temper. He pushed a hand through his hair and drew in a deep breath before continuing. "And you know yourself to be in perfect health? You're absolutely certain there is nothing you do not know about that could happen to you or the baby?"

He was almost shouting. Blair looked at him in surprise. *Where the heck had that come from?* Whatever, she was less than impressed. Before she could say a word, though, he reached for her hand, turning it over and stroking his thumb across the soft skin at the indentation of her palm.

"I'm sorry, I didn't mean to shout. But I do insist that you see a specialist. This baby—you—deserve the very best of care. I do not want to take any risks or have any last-minute emergencies that could have been avoided."

Blair felt the tingle under her skin at his touch, heard the depth of feeling in his words. For whatever reason, Draco was privately terrified. While she had to admit to some fears of her own, it came as a surprise to realize that he too felt vulnerable.

Draco continued to stroke Blair's palm. Her expression left him in no doubt that she was surprised by his outburst. Perhaps he'd gone over the top just now, but she hadn't been through what he'd been through. And he had every intention of making certain she didn't. Whether she agreed or not.

Eleven

Her emotions played across her face—irritation followed by surprise, then something else. He didn't have to wait long to discover what that something else was.

"Fine. I'll agree to see your specialist, if, and only if, you agree to let me take lessons from Cristiano while I'm here. I won't get in his way or impede his work, but I need to keep fresh and learning new dishes to take back to Carson's when I leave."

He forced himself to stifle the surge of anger that rose as she talked about when she would leave. She'd been here just over a day, and it was as if she had begun the count down to her return to New Zealand. Still, what would it cost him to let her dabble in the kitchen? It would keep her exactly where he wanted her, and once her pregnancy was common knowledge among all the staff, not just the maid he'd assigned to her, she would be cosseted and prevented from overdoing things.

Draco found himself nodding in acquiescence.

"And the gym too. I want unrestricted access to the equipment. Restaurant work is more physically demanding than many people realize. I can't afford to get soft."

"If the specialist is in agreement, then yes, you can use the gym too. I will hire a trainer for you so we can ensure you and the baby work out safely."

He was rewarded with a sudden smile.

"There, that didn't hurt too much, did it?" she teased him. "Letting me have what I want?"

A pain settled in the region of his chest. Why could she not want what he wanted? Why did she persist in holding on to her ambitions for Carson's? Certainly it was easy to agree to her terms, provided she saw the specialist for the duration of the pregnancy. Her health, and that of the baby's, was paramount. But while a child could cope easily with one parent, two would be infinitely better. Was it selfish to want his son or daughter to know the love of a mother and father as he and Lorenzo had known love as they'd grown up? He did not think so.

Somewhere deep inside he'd hoped that in the next few months he could convince Blair to let go of Carson's, but if she insisted on continuing to train in her field, what chance did he have?

The remainder of the week fell into a gentle pattern. Blair and Draco would have breakfast together before he'd head away for business for the day, sometimes returning at lunchtime to show her around parts of the palazzo or further afield. She'd thoroughly enjoyed their trip to San Gimignano and had marveled over the remaining towers there and the variety of shops and vendors in the narrow streets.

Blair's mornings, with her specialist's blessing, were spent in the gymnasium. Gabbi, the trainer Draco had hired to oversee her fitness regime, spoke excellent English, and the two women enjoyed one another's company for the two hours they spent together each day. Her workout, if it could be called that, was neither taxing nor exhausting, and Blair felt better and stronger each day.

Her afternoons were spent with Cristiano—time she cherished, as the kitchen was probably the only place in the palazzo where she truly felt at home. She was slowly building up a new collection of recipes and techniques to show off at the restaurant, although with each day, her return to Auckland seemed further and further away.

As Draco spent most of the afternoon and into early evening in his office, or visiting the various business units on the property, Blair had taken to having a leisurely swim in the heated pool in the hour or two before their evening meal. The rhythm of her life was so different from what she was used to, and day by day she could feel herself winding down.

She and Draco had not made love again since that time in the olive grove. She wasn't sure whether she should be bothered by that or not. She did feel a sense of loss each night, however, when after dinner he saw her to her room before continuing farther down the hall to his own suite.

One morning Blair noticed Draco appeared to be uncharacteristically distracted at breakfast.

"I may have to go away in the next few days," he announced. "There are matters in our London office that require my urgent attention, and I cannot deal with them from here."

"When will you know?" Blair asked, fidgeting with her linen serviette. As strange as it felt spending time with Draco this past week or so, it would feel a whole lot worse being here on her own. "We'll have to postpone our trip to Livorno, I suppose."

"Yes, I'm sorry. I wish it could be different. I had hoped not to have to travel again during the months you are here."

There it was, a reminder that she wouldn't be here for long. Confusion bubbled through her mind. Why did it bother her so much? She wanted to leave. As idyllic as her time here was, as stunning as the surroundings were, she ached to be home and back at Carson's. But she'd agreed to stay here, to have her baby here. Then, and only then, could she return home.

Her baby? When had she started thinking of it in those terms? Blair laid a hand gently on the small swell of her belly, still barely noticeable through her clothing but making its presence known in the number of jeans and shorts she was now incapable of fastening. So far, she'd managed to keep her mind pretty much off the baby, to keep any thoughts purely based on the fact that it was Draco's child. But something had happened along the way. Suddenly it was her baby as well.

Could she do it when the time came? *Leave her child? Leave the man she loved?*

Blair's eyes shot up to the man seated across the table. *Loved? Oh, my God,* she thought, a faint tremor rippling through her body. *She did love him.*

Every cell in her body was attuned to him. Her days became better, brighter, when he was with her. Life before him compared to life now, was like the difference between tinned spaghetti and the deliciously delicate flavors of porcini mushrooms and date shell mussels in the Spaghetti Allo Scoglio Cristiano had shown her the day before.

And that in itself was a perfect example of how she felt. On the outside looking in on perfection, yet not permitted inside.

She ached to see him each morning and missed him each night when they parted. Somehow, sometime in their tumultuous relationship, attraction had deepened, had turned into something more. Or perhaps, she realized, she had loved him all along but had fought tooth and nail to deny her own feelings. After all, her experience with Rhys had led to disaster, both emotional and financial, and her father's views on life and love had long tainted her own—making her distrustful, careful not to commit to anyone fully. In hindsight, that had probably been what had driven Rhys into Alicia's arms, Blair realized. Could she dare to hope that with Draco things could be different?

It would mean taking a chance, the biggest risk she'd ever taken in her life. Was she capable of such a thing?

"Is something wrong?" Draco asked, bringing his cup of coffee to his lips.

Blair shook her head, she barely trusted herself to

speak. Since the day they'd made love, Draco had been withdrawn from her. Sure, he remained friendly, a perfect host in fact. But he'd withdrawn from her emotionally. Different from the man she'd spent time with here, and again back in Auckland. One throwaway remark, cast by her in anger and shock when he'd discovered the pregnancy, had hardened him and created a gulf between them she had to decide to bridge or forever leave as a yawning chasm. The afternoon after they'd arrived here he'd let down his guard around her, and for the space of a few hours they'd recreated the bond they had between them.

But then she'd somehow damaged that closeness and he'd withdrawn back behind the demands of his work. Granted, they were many and spanned the globe—but they'd lost something she hadn't even known they'd shared, until it was gone. The loss—now she acknowledged it—had a left a gaping darkness deep inside her.

"I'll see you this evening then," he said, settling the fine china of his cup back on its saucer and rising from his seat.

"You won't be back at lunchtime?"

"Unfortunately not. I have business in Firenze today, but I'll be back in time for dinner."

"Florence? Could I come with you? It wouldn't take me a moment to get ready." She'd love the opportunity to find herself some new clothes and to poke around the culinary shops.

"Perhaps next time. I'll be tied up in meetings all day and I have no wish for you to get lost on your own."

"Draco, I'm a big girl. I can look after myself for the day."

"I'd rather show you the city when we have time to really enjoy it, and I'd like to see it through your eyes when I take you there for your first time."

Blair's heart somersaulted in her chest when he smiled at her. She swallowed back the disappointment that flooded her as he left the room, the disappointment and the ridiculous sense of abandonment she suddenly felt. Today was no different than any other, she scolded herself. She'd get ready now for her session with Gabbi and then enjoy the rest of the day as she'd enjoyed every other so far. So what if she had to amuse herself for lunch before her lesson with Cristiano? As she'd said to Draco, she was a big girl now, and besides, she had an awful lot she needed to think about before she saw him again.

Blair completed another lap of the pool, relishing the smooth glide of the water along her skin. She was no further ahead in her ponderings than she'd been this morning, in fact her concentration had been so off all day that even Cristiano had begun to lose a little patience with her in the kitchen this afternoon. In the end, she'd withdrawn from his domain pleading tiredness, and had enjoyed an unaccustomed afternoon nap in the shade here by the pool. She'd woken feeling fuzzy in the head. A fuzziness that was dissipating with each stroke of her arms as she turned and swam another length.

Blair's hands bumped against the edge of the pool and she stood ready to pull herself up and onto the edge. Suddenly she realized she wasn't alone.

On a lounger at the poolside sat an impeccably groomed woman. Blair didn't have to look hard to reognize a family resemblance. If she wasn't mistaken, this was Draco's mother. The woman rose and walked with a graceful stride toward her, offering a hand to Blair to help her out of the pool.

"Here, my dear. Let me assist you."

"Thank you." Blair took her hand, wishing like crazy that she'd opted today to wear her full-piece swimsuit. The bikini she'd slipped on did little to hide the thickening of her waist, and the new fullness to her breasts made her old bikini top almost indecent.

She accepted the thick, white towel the woman handed to her and wrapped it protectively around her, but the assessing look in the other woman's eye proved she had missed nothing.

"You must be Blair," she said, with a gentle smile. "I am Sabina Sandrelli, Draco's mother."

"I'm sorry, I wasn't expecting anyone," Blair started.

"I should have called first, I know. But I grow tired of waiting for Draco to introduce us. It is as I expected. You are pregnant, are you not?"

Blair felt color rush to her face. "I…"

"Don't worry, I am happy for the news, although it would have been nicer to have been told by my son than to have confirmed it myself." Sabina leaned forward and gave Blair a pat on her arm. "Umberto, Draco's father, will also be pleased. He tried to talk me out of bringing us both here today, but Draco has had long enough to keep you to himself. It was past time for you to meet the family, such as we are left."

"Draco's father is here also?" Blair asked, her eyes darting around to see if he was here at the poolside.

Sabina smiled. "He's in the kitchen, no doubt driving Cristiano crazy picking from his pots and pans to see what's for dinner. I heard the company helicopter come in a short while ago. Why don't you run along and get dressed and we can welcome Draco home together."

Without waiting for a response Sabina walked away, her elegant cream trousers and matching jacket fluttering gently in the light breeze that chased around the poolside patio. Blair slowly sank into the lounger Sabina had been sitting on. Draco's mother—*wow, that was an experience.* Clearly the woman was used to taking charge—*like mother, like son,* she thought ruefully, and reached for the sarong-style wrap she'd brought down to the pool with her. She wrapped it around her and wished that for once she'd had the presence of mind to grab a robe or something that would cover her more efficiently.

By the time she'd quickly showered and dried herself off, she started to worry about what on earth she could wear tonight that still fit. From the quality of Sabina Sandrelli's clothing and the way she carried herself, Blair had no doubt that she would expect her to dress for dinner. She'd decided on a pair of wide-legged elastic-waist pants and a loose-fitting top, but when she went through to her room there were two boxes sitting on her bed, with a brief handwritten note from Draco.

"I thought of you when I saw these."

She lifted the top off the first box and parted the tissue wrapped around its contents. A sigh gushed past her lips as she lifted out an exquisite mint-green nightgown, so sheer as to almost be indecent. He'd thought of her when he'd seen this? Perhaps there was hope for

her after all. The next layer revealed a matching peignoir. Blair held the gossamer-fine garments against her
skin. She couldn't wait to wear them, but somehow she
doubted that this would be the kind of thing that the
elegant Sabina had been expecting.

Blair removed the top off the second box and pulled
out a cobalt-blue gown. She held it against her and
swirled in front of the mirror. The color did amazing
things for her skin, she decided, and the design—a full
skirt dropping from the wide Empire-style waistband—
would be perfect not only now, but in the coming
summer months too. She dressed quickly and slid her
feet into high-heeled black pumps.

A knock at the door dragged her from the mirror
where she'd been standing, admiring the fall of the gown.

"Ah, it looks even better on you than on the model,"
Draco said, coming into her room and closing the door.

Her eyes feasted on him. Dressed in a tailored,
charcoal-gray suit, he was both formidable and undeni-
ably sexy. Suddenly Blair felt self-conscious. She
plucked at the fabric of dress.

"Thank you, it's beautiful," she said softly. "It's all
lovely."

"I'm glad. I notice you haven't worn earrings since
you've been here, yet your ears are pierced. I hope you
don't mind, but I bought you these."

Draco withdrew a small jeweler's box from his jacket
pocket and opened it. All the breath in Blair's lungs froze
when she saw the platinum-set diamond ear studs there.

"May I?" Draco asked.

He put the box down on the table next to him, then

gently slipped one earring from its nest and removed the butterfly clasp off the back. His fingers brushed against Blair's neck, his touch setting a flame across her skin as he put first one earring in one lobe, then the other. He turned her to face the mirror.

Blair lifted a trembling hand to touch an earring. She'd never owned anything so valuable before. As she reviewed her reflection, she almost didn't recognize the woman who'd returned to the palazzo just over a week ago. There was a bloom to her skin that spoke of her increasing health, and the skin under her eyes was clear of the usual shadow of tiredness. In the gown and with these earrings she could almost fool herself into believing she belonged here amongst the sumptuous furnishings, at the side of the impeccably attired man reflected beside her. But she knew that was little more than a futile dream.

"Thank you, Draco, they're beautiful. But I can't accept such an expensive gift. Really."

Regret sliced through her as she spoke from her heart. No matter what her trappings, she'd still be Blair Carson, chef and restaurateur. That title, and Carson's, were what defined her. It was what she was, pure and simple.

"They are yours to do with what you wish, it makes no difference to me." The warm light that had been in his eyes dimmed a little. "Now, shall we join my parents downstairs?"

Blair had almost forgotten. Almost, but not quite. Butterflies danced nervously in her stomach.

"She knows, Draco. Your mother, she knows I'm pregnant. She guessed."

"I expected as much. Don't worry. It is not a problem."

Blair fervently hoped it wouldn't be, and that she wouldn't be put on the spot by Draco's parents over their relationship. Tonight promised to be awkward. Already, she was looking forward to its end.

Downstairs they joined Sabina and Umberto in the formal salon Blair had only glimpsed from the doorway in the past week.

"Ah, don't you look lovely," Draco's mother said, rising from her chair and crossing the room to take Blair by the hand. "Umberto, come meet Blair."

Draco's father was clearly a shadow of the man he'd once been, one side of his body clearly difficult to move and control. Once the introductions were completed, Sabina drew Blair to one side of the room, seating her by one of the tall, arched windows and taking the chair opposite.

"We can leave the men to their business. If they get it out of the way now, they won't disturb us with it over our meal," she said conspiratorially.

Blair just smiled. There was something about Sabina that made her feel inadequate. Nothing obvious, just a sensation. She was probably being ridiculous, but as Sabina gently prompted Blair for information about herself and her family, she felt as if she was sinking deeper and deeper in the other woman's estimation.

Technically, she supposed she should be the hostess in this situation, but she knew that Sabina had spent most of her married life here in the palazzo, only moving to a smaller villa on the property a couple of years ago. Her general air of command put Blair very much on the defensive—a position she didn't enjoy.

"Tell me, when is the baby due?" Sabina asked once she'd plumbed the depths of Blair's family tree. Something that hadn't taken very long.

"Not until the middle of November," Blair managed to say through stiff lips.

"Ah, a winter baby. The nursery here is well-insulated, so you will not have to concern yourself that he will be cold."

"There is a nursery?" Blair blurted out before she could think.

Of course there'd be a nursery here. Generations of Sandrellis had been born here so it made perfect sense the children would have had their own accommodation. A pang of concern struck her. Despite her agreement with Draco, she didn't want to leave her baby. The very thought now filled her with dread.

"Men!" Sabina rolled her eyes. "I cannot believe that Draco has not shown you the nursery. After dinner I will show it to you. Now, tell me more about yourself. How did you and my son meet?"

Sabina was a great listener, and before long Blair had told her not only about how they'd met but how Draco had come back into her life in New Zealand. The older woman was nodding with a smile on her face.

"That's my son. Never one to stand back and wait when he can just take what he wants. But despite that, he's a good boy."

Blair fought back a grin, it was hard to imagine that anyone could refer to Draco as a "boy." As far as she was concerned he was all man—and it made the current distance between them all the harder to bear. She missed the closeness they'd shared before he discovered the pregnancy. As Sabina waxed lyrical about her son's achievements, Blair gained a new insight into the complexities of the man she loved. It was clear he would do anything for his parents, and that despite the fact his father was no longer capable of being active in the Sandrelli's business affairs, he regularly consulted with him about business decisions.

"Of course, when Marcella died we were all devastated. Umberto and I are very happy he's found another so special."

Sabina's words made Blair sit upright. "Marcella?"

"Ah, I see Draco hasn't told you about her yet." Sabina's lips formed a moue of irritation and she sighed. "Well, now, since I've mentioned her name, I should probably put your curiosity to rest."

"I'm not—"

"My dear, don't worry. Curiosity is a good thing, and if you and my son are to be married, then you should know about his late fiancée."

Married? Before Blair could disabuse Draco's mother of the idea another word sank into her head. *Fiancée?*

"It was terribly sad, of course. Marcella was such a darling girl. No one knew about her heart defect."

"Had they…had they known each other long?"

Blair both wanted to know about this other woman and didn't. She knew she'd be found wanting if she was to be compared side-by-side with the woman he had loved enough to offer marriage.

"Oh yes, she was the daughter of old friends. We'd always hoped for a family alliance, but sadly, it wasn't meant to be." Sabina lapsed into silence for a moment before continuing. "It's why I wanted to see you for myself, you know. I suspected, when Draco told me you were living here, that you were more than just one of his passing flings. Then when I saw you, I knew you must be pregnant. I'm so glad he now has the chance to have the child he lost when Marcella passed away."

"She was pregnant?" A cold chill ran down Blair's back.

"Yes, she knew how important family was to Draco, especially after Lorenzo's accident. She didn't want to wait until after they were married to start their family. Of course her parents were horrified when she announced to us all that she was having Draco's baby, but they soon came to look forward to it as much as we did."

"You mentioned a heart problem. Did Marcella know?"

"Apparently so. She'd been warned not to have children, but I think she was scared she'd lose Draco if she didn't. She risked her life to have his baby. Sadly, the risk was too great. We lost them both. I thought Draco would go mad with grief."

Again Sabina lapsed into silence, but then drew in a deep breath and straightened her shoulders.

"But that's in the past, and now we have a new baby to look forward to. And a wedding!" She clapped her hands together. "Have you two set a date yet?"

"No, Mamma, we have not."

Both women wheeled around in their seats as Draco's voice interrupted them. He handed his mother a glass of white wine and Blair a fruit juice. Blair couldn't tell from his expression whether he'd overheard his mother's conversation. Draco speared her with a searching glance. Did he imagine for one minute that she'd told his mother they were engaged? Blair knew she had to put Sabina right.

"Actually, we're not engaged," she said, slightly breathless.

"Not engaged?" Sabina's perfect eyebrows shot toward her hairline and she directed a stern look at her son.

"No, Mamma," Draco confirmed in a voice that did not encourage further discussion on the topic.

His father shuffled over to join them and conversation turned to more general topics, but all evening and all through their meal Blair was plagued with questions racing around in her mind about his dead fiancée.

Suddenly, Draco's heavy-handed approach to her pregnancy began to make sense now. She had a deeper understanding of what this pregnancy meant to him, why his reaction had been so sudden and so severe when he'd found out about it, and why he was so determined she have the best care that money could buy. Not that it had saved poor Marcella, she thought grimly. She wondered what had driven the other woman to deliberately enter into a pregnancy, knowing it could take her life—take her from the very man she loved enough to want to spend the rest of her life with him.

For a moment, Blair allowed herself the luxury of envy of Marcella—of the fact that she had loved Draco and been loved in return. But then she felt ashamed. Jealous of a dead woman? That was taking herself to a new low indeed.

That Draco already loved their unborn baby Blair had no doubt; but she knew that love couldn't extend to her as well. It was ironic. The last time she'd believed herself in love with a man, her best friend had come between them. This time it was a baby and the memory of Marcella. How could she ever hope to compete with that?

At least she had Carson's. It was the one constant in her life and would be waiting for her when all this was over. She had to hold onto that thought. It was the only thing that would get her through all of this.

She wanted more than that, though. She wanted Draco. She wanted what he'd shared with Marcella, together with all the hopes and dreams for the future. The idea terrified her and exhilarated her at the same time. She fingered the charm bracelet she'd worn since the day he'd given it to her, and considered the earrings he'd put in her ears himself this evening. He wasn't totally uncaring of her. Maybe, just maybe, they could make it work.

It was late when Umberto and Sabina left to return to their villa and Blair let herself into her bedroom. During the tour of the nursery with Sabina, Blair had expressed surprise that, with the size of the palazzo, Draco's parents didn't keep a suite of rooms here. But Sabina had explained that all her married life she'd done what had been expected of her in the Sandrelli name. Now that Draco had taken over the reins from his father, it was time for them to truly be a couple and have their own home and their own dreams together. And besides, with his disabilities from a series of small strokes, Umberto was far more comfortable in their single-level dwelling.

Sabina's comments had struck a chord with Blair. Despite Sabina's hopes that the men would confine their business discussions to their predinner drinks, the dinner table had been dominated by Sandrelli affairs. She could understand why the other woman would have wanted some distance between work and home life, but it was her compassion and obvious love for her husband that struck a deeper chord.

It was clear to her that Sabina was very much still the lady of the palazzo. She'd given up all of this so her husband wouldn't need to struggle or rely on others for what independence he still held.

Again it occurred to Blair that Draco would have very little time for their baby, once it was born. She had to find some way to heal the rift between them and span their differences. She couldn't bear the idea that their child would be raised by a succession of nannies if she failed to convince Draco of her need to now be a part in their baby's life.

Blair may not have had her mother's love growing up, and her father had been focused on his work a lot of the time, but he'd been there for her one way or another. And she wanted to be there for the baby too.

Blair had to talk to Draco. Tonight, before her courage deserted her. She had to convince him to consider a future between them.

Carefully, she took off the blue dress Draco had bought her and placed it on a hanger, then she removed her underwear and slid the nearly translucent nightgown and peignoir on over skin that had suddenly become hypersensitive to the silky-soft texture of the garment. She tangled her fingers through her hair and pinched at cheeks that had suddenly paled.

That would have to do, she thought, and before she could change her mind, she let herself out the room and padded on bare feet down the hall to Draco's suite. Without hesitating, she rapped her knuckles on his door and, not even waiting for his reply, opened it and stepped inside.

Twelve

"Is there something wrong?"

Draco turned from the desk where he'd been standing, reading a sheet of paper. He placed the paper and the cut crystal tumbler he'd held in his hand on the glossy wooden surface of the desk and crossed the distance between them, concern pulling his eyebrows into a frown.

"No, I'm fine, I just wanted to talk to you a while. That's all."

Now that she was here, she suddenly felt nervous. She shouldn't have changed into the nightgown that was for sure. While it had seemed a good idea at the time, right now she felt as if she'd put herself on display, when what she wanted was Draco's total attention—and not in *that* way.

"The night wear looks lovely on you."

Appreciation gleamed in Draco's eyes, and Blair felt her body warm and stir under his gaze.

"Thank you," she said, her words a little breathless.

She averted her eyes and sat down on one of the comfortable, overstuffed couches in his sitting room and cleared her throat.

"Your mother spoke to me about a few things today," she started.

"I can imagine," Draco said with a smile. "My mother generally has much to say on every topic."

"She told me about Marcella." There, she'd said it. The other woman's name had slid off her tongue without so much as a hint of the envy she unrealistically bore his dead fiancée.

Draco's eyes narrowed into cold, emerald chips. "What, exactly, did my mother tell you?"

Maybe this was a mistake. Blair smoothed an imaginary wrinkle from her sleeve and drew in another breath before speaking.

"She told me you were engaged and that Marcella died while she was pregnant, before you could be married."

"And?"

Blair shot him a look. His expression gave nothing away. If he still bore any love for Marcella it wasn't evident on his features.

"I…I wondered if you could tell me about her. It might help me to understand a bit better."

"Understand?" Draco paced the floor in front of her. "What is to understand? My life with Marcella has nothing to do with you and me. Marcella loved me, we were engaged to be married, and yes, she was pregnant with my child when she died of a heart defect she'd neglected to inform me of. Had I known—"

Draco broke off and swore volubly in Italian. He stopped his pacing and came to a halt in front of Blair.

"Had you known?" she prompted, wishing she hadn't embarked on this conversation. To hear him talk of Marcella—to talk of love—could only flay her fragile heart. What the heck had she been thinking?

Draco sighed, a violent huff of air from his lungs that spoke volumes about his emotional frustration.

"Had I known, I would have been more careful. She would not have become pregnant. We would have married and grown old together. It would have been enough."

"Perhaps she didn't believe that. Perhaps she knew how important your family was to you. And with your brother gone, she felt she had no choice."

"Choice? She gave me no choice. She knew her weak heart would never sustain a pregnancy, yet she never shared that information with me at any time."

"I'm sorry, Draco. Losing her must have been hell for you."

"Hell for me and for my parents. They had been looking forward to the baby so much. After Lorenzo's death, a piece of them died too. Knowing Marcella was pregnant brought so much joy and anticipation to their lives. But that was destroyed when she died. Tell me, Blair, how is a man supposed to go on when the woman he loves holds such a truth from him, and by doing so takes not only her life but the life of his child?"

Words stuck in Blair's throat at the raw grief so evident in Draco's question.

"I was everything to Marcella. She was devoted to me, and it cost her life. Is that what you wanted to know? She would never have put work ahead of me and the baby, especially not the baby."

Blair's back stiffened. "Is that some sort of criticism of me?"

"Take it however you want to," Draco responded wearily. "But at least be honest with yourself. I know you could never love another person as much as Marcella loved me, or be as self-sacrificing, because you only have one priority in your life—your precious restaurant. But that doesn't matter. At least you are honest about it and you and I both know exactly where we stand. Besides, we both know that you have no intention of being a real mother to the child."

Blair jerked as if he'd slapped her.

"And tell me, Draco. Just when in your business schedule do you think you'll have time to be a *real* father? I barely see you. So, what kind of parent will you be? You're so quick to criticize my desire to have a successful career, but maybe you should look at yourself first."

She was shaking with reaction, as first fury, then something else coursed through her body. She didn't want to think about how she felt right now, but all that ran through her mind was the truth that he would never consider a long-term future with her. Her thoughts were backed up by his next words.

"My duty will always lie first and foremost with my family. Don't ever doubt that. I will be there for this baby—far more than you—so before you start flinging rocks at me you should check you are not standing in a glass house. You've made it clear that your career is worth more to you than a relationship with your child or with me. Even now, every day, you work toward your goal of returning to your kitchen."

Blair couldn't deny it. Every day she took lessons with Cristiano, but the past couple of days her enthusiasm for translating the recipes into the menu at Carson's had waned a little. In her nightly calls to her father, he'd gone to great lengths to say how he was coping brilliantly with the workload. In fact, she hadn't heard him sound as happy and fulfilled in a long time. It still concerned her that he hadn't yet appointed a new chef, but she consoled herself that it was only a matter of time.

"At least I have a goal," she responded staunchly, grasping at straws to bolster her flagging self-esteem. "I'm not solely allowing myself to be defined by the man I'm with or by our children."

Draco grew still, and Blair knew she'd gone too far.

"I pity you," Draco said through gritted teeth. "I pity you that you can lower yourself to insult a woman who was a saint in comparison to you. A woman who gave her life for what she thought *I* wanted. Remember yourself, Blair. You chose this course of events. You chose to be no more than the vessel that will bring security to the Sandrelli name and happiness to my family, rather than be a part of it. And when you have delivered on that promise you will go back to your restaurant and our lives will continue as they have for centuries."

Ice poured through Blair's veins. He couldn't have put it more bluntly. He and his family belonged here in a way she never could. They were a part of the land, a part of the people, a part of each other in a way she'd never known and never would. At least her baby would have that, be part of that.

She blinked back the tears that burned like embers against the back of her eyes. She'd been a fool to think she could come here and talk to Draco about a future together. It would never have worked anyway. She was probably just mushy-brained because of this pregnancy—wooed into the lifestyle and surroundings and dreams of what she could never have or be.

Summoning all the dignity she could muster, Blair rose from her seat. The soft folds of fabric of her nightgown and peignoir settled around her body like a lover's caress, and she shuddered to think that, if things could have been different between herself and Draco, he would no doubt have been removing the garments by now.

But instead of making plans for a new future she clung to every last shred of what she had left. She lifted her chin and met Draco's glittering gaze head on.

"Thank you for the reminder. You're right. Of course. To be honest, I can't wait for all this," she gestured to her belly "to be over so I can get back to my life."

She saw Draco's jaw clench, noticed the muscle working on the side of his face. She'd struck him a blow, but she'd struck one equally as deep to her own heart.

She'd fallen in love with a man who would always put others—their child, his family—ahead of her. Just for once in her life, she'd ached to be first in a man's life; but she could never hope to be that person with Draco.

She forced one foot in front of the other until she reached the door, then gripped the handle and turned it sharply. Every cell in her body urged her to stop, to turn and look back at Draco. To see if he showed one hint of softening toward her, one chance to change his mind about her and the baby. But men like Draco took their responsibilities too seriously to ever be that yielding.

With her back still to him she said bitterly, "I feel sorry for you, Draco. At least I'm moving on with my life. You? You're still locked in the past…"

She pulled the door closed behind her and staggered to her bedroom, and once inside, she ripped off the peignoir and nightgown, hearing the fabric shred as she sought to rid herself of its softness, its sensuality—its reminder of all it was and all she wasn't. With shaking hands she removed the diamond ear studs Draco had given her, and unsnapped the clasp on the charm bracelet. She needed none of it. They were trappings of someone else. Someone she could never be. She was Blair Carson, chef and restaurateur, and damned proud of it.

And that's what she kept reminding herself as she tugged on an old T-shirt and slid beneath the covers of her bed. She and her baby didn't need anyone or anything else. Ever. And certainly not Draco Sandrelli.

The next few days dragged out interminably for Blair. Draco was cool and distant, and on those rare occasions they crossed paths, it was painfully clear that every last vestige of the camaraderie they'd tentatively shared was wiped from their existence.

Blair threw herself into her lessons with new enthusiasm; she needed something—anything—to keep her focused on her future. The time she spent in the kitchen and scouring the markets with Cristiano became a salve to her wounded soul, so much so that, when she sensed a tiny flutter of movement in the pit of her stomach one morning, it took her completely by surprise. At only fifteen weeks pregnant, she knew it was early by most standards to sense any movement of the baby, and initially she shrugged the bubbling sensation off as something else. But when it happened again she couldn't be so sure.

She pressed a hand to her belly and waited for the sensation again, yet nothing happened. But later that night, as she settled into bed, she became aware of the sensation again. Tears pricked at her eyes as she stroked her hand against her belly again—suddenly, irrevocably, connecting with her baby in a way she'd never thought she'd experience. *How different things could have been if only she could share this with Draco,* she thought, as she let hot tears glide down her cheeks.

The next morning, she was surprised to see Draco in the kitchen waiting for her. They'd barely spoken more than a half dozen words to one another since the night his parents had come to dinner.

"I will be leaving for London as soon as the jet is ready," he informed her. "But I will be back in time to take you to the doctor for your sixteen-week checkup."

"It doesn't matter if you're not back yet. I can go on my own," Blair stated baldly. In fact, she'd prefer it if he didn't come, so strained had they been around one another lately.

"I said I will be back in time, and I will. I keep to my word, Blair. You'd do well to remember that."

Blair flung a look at Cristiano, who had his back to

them as he sprinkled sage into the omelet he was preparing for her breakfast, and blushed. She hated that Draco felt he could speak to her like this in front of one of his staff.

"Whatever." She shrugged. "It doesn't matter to me either way."

It was petty and childish, she knew, to have answered him back like that, but his stiff, overbearing manner with her made her feel like a child. She sat at the table and pushed her eggs around on her plate, tension drawing a tight line across the back of her shoulders until she felt him move away and out the room.

She heard the revving engine of his car as he sped away from the palazzo and down the private road that led to the airfield, and deep inside of her a part of her wept that they had come to this.

By the end of the week, Blair was becoming used to the occasional tiny flutter that signaled the baby's movement. Granted, the sensations were still slight, but for the first time in ages she didn't feel so alone. She'd heard nothing from Draco in the time he'd been gone. Given her parting comment to him, it was no great surprise. She'd expected to feel more relaxed at the palazzo without him here, but instead she felt like an intruder. As if she didn't belong. And she didn't, not really. As he'd so succinctly put it that awful night, she was here to deliver. And once she did, she'd be heading back home.

Blair had been in the kitchen garden, picking a little flat-leaf parsley to add to the potato croquettes she was experimenting with, when she heard the distant peal of the telephone. Since Draco had left, the phone had hardly rung at all, and for a moment she felt her heart leap with anticipation that he might be calling her. As she entered the kitchen, she eschewed the idea. He was no more likely to call her than he was about to drop on bended knee and ask her to stay.

She shook her head slightly, castigating herself for being a fool. But to be honest with herself, she was missing him terribly. It was hard to admit that she wanted him here, with her. She, who needed no one, apparently needed him a whole lot more than she'd ever realized.

"*Signorina!* The telephone. It is for you," one of the maids came rushing through to the kitchen, gesturing to the wall phone.

"Thank you." Blair smiled.

Butterflies took flight in her stomach. Was she wrong? Could it be Draco?

The voice at the other end of the phone soon put that thought out of her head.

"Ms. Carson, my name is Doctor Featherstone, from Auckland City Hospital. Your father has been admitted with a heart attack. He's stable at present, and we will need to operate. But he appears to be more concerned about his restaurant than his health. He refuses to consent to the surgery. Quite frankly, if we don't operate he won't be so lucky the next time around."

Blair's head swam. *A heart attack? Oh God, no!* She should never have left. She should have known he'd take on all the responsibility of the restaurant and refuse to hire another chef, or even share more of the workload with the sous chef. This was all her fault—and Draco's.

"Can I speak with him?" she managed through lips that felt numb.

"He's sedated at present, but I can pass a message on."

"Please, tell him not to worry about Carson's. I'll be on the next plane home. Tell him I'll take care of things. All he needs to do is get well again."

She took a few details from the doctor, then hung up the phone and sank against the wall. A heart attack. She closed her eyes and drew in a shuddering breath. She could have lost her father, and all because Draco insisted on her having his baby here in his beloved Tuscany. Well, as far as Blair was concerned, where the baby was born was neither here nor there anymore. Her father needed her, and, as Draco was so fond of pointing out to her, family came first.

Her duty to her father was no less than his to his family, celebrated history or not.

She pulled her ragged thoughts together and picked up the telephone to dial Information. She had to get home as quickly as possible. Her father's health, even his life, depended on it.

Thirteen

By the time Blair staggered up the stairs to the flat above the restaurant she was shattered. The irony of flying from Rome to London and then making a connecting flight via Hong Kong to Auckland wasn't lost on her. Briefly, she'd been in the same city as Draco and he hadn't even known it. With the number of time zones she'd been through, she felt as if she'd been traveling for days, even if it had only been something over thirty hours. But she was here. Home. Where she was needed and wanted.

It was nearing lunchtime, but all she wanted was to fall into bed and sleep. She made a quick call to the hospital and asked to be put through to her dad, but her call was intercepted by a nurse who told her he was resting comfortably. Blair left a brief message with the nurse for her father, disappointed she couldn't speak to him. She'd only be able to manage a few hours' sleep before she'd need to be on deck downstairs. Calling him again would have to wait until morning. But still, he'd know she was here and taking care of things, and now he could consent to the surgery that would keep him with her longer.

Aside from the weariness of her first day back, Blair fell back into the rhythm and routine of Carson's with a comfort and familiarity she'd always taken for granted. Her father had been scheduled for surgery later in the week and, all going well, he could expect a strong recovery—although he'd never be up to the strain of working at the pace required to keep Carson's at the peak of its popularity.

Two days later, at the end of her shift, Blair made her way upstairs and gratefully sank into the sagging sofa bed she didn't quite have the energy to pull out and climb into properly. She kicked off her shoes and wiggled her toes.

Despite some swelling in her feet and legs at the end of her shift, she was managing just fine with being back in a busy working kitchen. Although she was coping, it still felt as though something was missing for her. The thrill and excitement of the restaurant's hectic pace didn't fire her up and motivate her as much as it had done in the past.

She'd grown soft at the palazzo, she decided. But that didn't explain the ache in her heart, or the sense that something far more important in her world was missing. She told herself it was only to be expected. She was in love with a man who only saw her as some sort of brood-mare, even if that situation was pretty much of her own making. It was no wonder she was a little deflated—okay, maybe a lot deflated. With the travel, followed by immers-ing herself straight back into work and the worry about her father's health, she was entitled to feel a little down.

She wondered if Draco had returned to the palazzo yet. She had no doubt he'd be livid when he discovered her gone. Maybe he'd even sell the restaurant building out from under her. Right now though, she couldn't care less. Her first priority was to her dad, and in making sure he got through his surgery with flying colors, and the only way to do that was to keep the restaurant humming.

Carson's maintained its five-star rating on the *Fine Dining* magazine site, but somehow the accolade seemed hollow. It was, after all, one person's opinion. Why had it been so important to her, when now it barely mattered at all? In all the years her father had run Carson's he'd strived for that rating, and during the time they worked together it had become their joint dream. Then, when her father had retired, Blair had assumed the goal as her own—pushing herself and her staff to greater heights to reach that ever-elusive award.

And what for? For something her father had wanted? For something that had ruled his life, determined his cre-ativity? Measured the man and the chef he was? Even though their earlier years had been transient, he'd always been sought after. Was she so driven to be just like him that she'd lost sight of what she was—what she wanted?

All her years growing up, she'd craved the stability of a secure home and a steady income and she had that here with Carson's. Or did she? Blair had dared to hope for love, had dared to believe that she could blend her career with marriage, and maybe one day, a family.

Or maybe, she thought as she compared herself to her father's single state, she'd allowed her father's dreams and goals to set the course for her life at the expense of her own. She bent down and massaged her aching feet, wishing, not for the first time, that she had a partner to do this for her. No, someone more than a partner. More than she'd ever allowed Rhys to be. She wanted a soul mate. Someone without whom life was empty, someone with whom the stars shone that much brighter in the sky at night and the world was a brighter and happier place.

Blair shook her head at her fanciful thoughts and changed feet. The closest thing she'd have to a partner right now was her relationship with a foot spa that she was invariably too tired to lug out of the cupboard and set up to soothe her tired feet.

She wondered how she was going to cope as she grew bigger, especially with her father unable to return to work. The doctor, this morning, had been adamant. If, after his surgery, he couldn't pace himself to a few hours a day, then he had to stay away from the restaurant completely. Blair made a mental note to advertise in the national newspaper for someone to share her role at the restaurant. She'd hoped Phil would be up to speed by now to take the promotion, but he had a wife and a toddler, with another baby on the way, and he'd made it clear when she'd broached the subject with him that he was happy where he was while his family was still so young.

She'd envied his wife in that moment more than she'd

ever believed possible. She tried not to think about it, but right now it pressed heavily on the back of her mind. What would happen to her after the baby was born? She had no doubt that Draco would insist on full custody, and, to be totally honest, she couldn't maintain her work pace and be a parent as well. She was between a rock and a hard place, and neither of them were where she really wanted to be.

"What do you mean she is gone?" Draco thundered, striding through the salon at the palazzo. "Why did no one tell me of this?"

"Ms. Carson said not to concern you, *signore.*"

The poor maid who'd informed him of Blair's defection looked as if she was on the verge of tears.

Concern? She didn't want him to be concerned? How ironic when she had been on his mind every second of every day, and he'd been in a fool's paradise, imagining her here at the palazzo. Safe. Secure.

"When did she leave?" he asked, pitching his voice lower, softer.

"Last Friday, *signore.*"

"Thank you, Maria, and I'm sorry for shouting at you."

His apology earned him a watery smile and another liberal dose of guilt. It went a long way toward showing how upset he was that he'd lost control with one of his staff. Draco looked at his watch—it was midday. The time in New Zealand would be around ten in the evening. Hopefully a good time to get hold of Blair at the restaurant—because he knew without a single doubt that was where she'd be.

Two hours later Draco snapped his phone off for what felt like the hundredth time. So, Blair was too busy to come to the phone and talk to him, was she? He'd see about that. He'd been shocked to hear that her father was in the hospital awaiting bypass surgery, but he didn't see why both Carsons needed to work themselves into early graves. His instructions to Blair's father had been explicit. That the man had ignored them and that Blair was now putting herself and their baby's health in jeopardy was enough to make Draco see a violent shade of red.

Draco swiftly punched in the phone number of Blair's apartment and left a message on the answering machine that would leave her with no doubt of his intentions.

"We had an agreement, Blair. I will do whatever it takes to make sure you stop working until my baby is born. Be sure of it, and expect to see me very soon."

The next morning Draco readied himself for the long flight back to New Zealand. For the number of times he'd used the charter jet recently, he may as well invest in one for himself, he decided, as one of his staff zipped his suitcase closed and took it down to the waiting car.

He stopped in Blair's room on his way back downstairs. He hadn't set foot in here since the day he'd returned from Firenze—when he'd given her the earrings and the clothes. A trace of her fragrance lingered in the air and he inhaled it deeply.

He hadn't wanted to admit it, or even to believe it, but he'd missed Blair terribly during his time in London. It had been a physical ache, permeating his body and his mind. Not calling her had been difficult to deal with, but they'd left on such awkward terms—what could he have said on the phone that shouldn't be said face-to-face? Yes, he'd missed her all right. Enough to realize how wrongly he'd treated her the night she'd asked about Marcella.

Wrongly? Hell. He'd been cruel. Deliberately deflecting his pain, his loss—his shortcomings—onto Blair.

But talking about Marcella had been like ripping the scab off a wound. And through it all he'd still been forced to beat back the desire that raged through him every time Blair was in his orbit. She'd sat there in that delicious concoction of night wear, her skin glowing translucent through the sheer folds of material, looking nothing like the woman he'd promised to marry, yet everything like the woman he loved.

The realization had been as painful as it had been eye-opening.

He had never loved Marcella as much as he knew he now loved Blair. What he'd felt for her was a pale comparison to the emotions that ripped through him now. And that made him feel even more guilty, if that was humanly possible—even more responsible for Marcella's death. She'd been prepared to do anything for him, even risk her life for what he wanted, and how had he repaid her? By working all the hours that God sent him, by being a fleeting fiancé at the best of times. And yet, she'd stuck by him, loved him when he hadn't deserved so much as an ounce of the measure of her love.

He hadn't been the man Marcella deserved, and he hadn't protected her as he ought to have, but one thing was certain. He would protect Blair and their unborn child with every last breath in his body, and that began with getting her back here, back home under his roof—and this time within the secure circle of his arms and his love.

Convincing Blair her place was at his side was going to take some doing. Carson's was in her blood, of that he was now convinced. Yes, he could understand her needing to return home to be at her father's side after his heart attack, but from what he'd understood from his brief conversations with her staff at the restaurant, she was busy in the kitchen for nearly all the hours available to her. A brief visit to her father each morning on her way home from the markets hardly counted, in Draco's mind. She was there for the restaurant. She measured everything she was by that place, and somehow it was more daunting for Draco to know he was fighting for her against some*thing*, rather than someone.

He spied the jewelry she'd left behind on the dresser. That small gesture as telling as if she'd graffiti-sprayed it on the wall. She wanted no part of him. Well, it was time for her to reconsider.

It was nearly two in the morning when Draco's jet touched down at Auckland International Airport. As the plane taxied to the private air terminal he itched to disembark, chafing at the delay created by the requirements to go through customs and immigration, however efficiently it was conducted. His driver waited for him in the terminal building and stepped forward to take Draco's bag and lead him to the waiting limousine.

Draco drummed his fingers on his leg as they seemed to get every red light on George Bolt Memorial Drive, on their way to the motorway link that would lead them into the city. It was far too late to show up at the apartment and talk to Blair right now, but he had every intention of being there first thing in the morning—before she headed to the hospital to see her father, and before he was taken into surgery.

He rested his head briefly on the leather headrest, but started as his cell phone chirped in his breast pocket. He identified the number as that of his second in command here in New Zealand and flipped open the phone.

"Sandrelli." His voice was clipped and cool in the confines of the luxury vehicle, but what he heard next struck fear into his heart and changed the tone and pitch of his voice in a split second.

"A fire? At Carson's. When? Has anyone been hurt?"

As his questions were answered in succession, Draco felt as if a giant hand had reached out and squeezed his heart. If the fire started in the kitchen, would Blair have had warning as she slept upstairs in her tiny apartment? Then he heard the news he'd been dreading.

Casualties.

Fire fighters struggling to contain the blaze.

The bad news came in a succession of blows, but none of it told him the information he most dreaded.

"Blair Carson. Where is she?" he demanded, his voice cracking on her name.

"I don't have any news of her yet, I'm sorry."

Draco closed his phone with a shaking hand and redirected his driver to Ponsonby. He had to get there and see for himself if Blair was all right. He wouldn't allow himself to think of anything but seeing her safe and well, because right now the alternative was, quite frankly, too terrifying to even consider.

Access to the road where Carson's sat was closed by snaking fire hoses across the bitumen and the organized chaos of emergency vehicles and personnel. Two ambulances stood at the head of the road, one closing its doors and racing away from the scene, siren screaming. Before the limousine had even rolled to a halt, Draco was out the door and racing toward the restaurant.

His eyes were drawn in horrified fascination to the beast of fire that, even with the hoses trained upon it, continued to consume the restaurant with unequalled appetite. A police officer approached him.

"Excuse me, sir, you'll have to stand back."

"Blair Carson. Do you know where Blair Carson is?"

A loud boom suddenly shook the air and a ball of fire shot skyward. Firefighters continued to train their hoses on the fire, but Draco could see already it was only a matter of confining the flames to Carson's and protecting the neighboring buildings. For the restaurant itself there was no hope.

He caught the look of pity that swept across the officer's face, and Draco felt as if the bottom had just dropped out of his world.

"Please," he demanded, "tell me where she is. Tell me she's not still in there."

"I'll see what I can find out for you, sir, but please, you must stand back."

The officer gave Draco a gentle shove and he took a couple of steps back, silently praying as he'd never prayed before.

Fourteen

How long he stood there on the side of the road he didn't know, but a sudden movement near the back of the remaining ambulance caught his eye.

Blair! She was all right.

He covered the distance between them in a matter of seconds, reaching to take her into his arms and to confirm for himself that she was okay. Her face was smudged with soot, her clothes also, and the indentation of an oxygen mask on her face left him in no doubt she'd been in terrible danger not so very long ago.

Blair batted away at his hands as he sought to touch her. Shoving hard at him when he tried again to hold her.

"How could you?" she rasped, her voice raw and tears tracking pale lines down her face. "Was this what you meant when you said you'd make me stop working? Was it?"

She was hysterical with grief.

"Blair, no. How could you think such a thing? I would never do something like this to you. Never," he answered vehemently.

She started to cough, and a burly paramedic came up beside her to gently urge her back, to sit on the back step of the ambulance. He placed the oxygen mask once again over her nose and mouth and spoke quietly to her for a moment. When he straightened up again Draco stepped forward.

"Why is she still here? Surely, she should be in hospital. She's sixteen weeks pregnant. Shouldn't she be checked out?"

"Ms. Carson has refused to go to hospital for assessment. I'm keeping her on oxygen for now."

"Is it true, Blair? Have you refused to go to the hospital?"

Tears continued to streak down her cheeks. Draco squatted down in front of her, taking her hands.

"*Cara mia,* you must see a doctor."

"I can't," her voice was muffled by the mask. "I can't go until it's over."

Her eyes were riveted on the conflagration that had been her pride, her home and her very life. Draco understood her need to be here, even though his every instinct screamed at him to bundle her into the back of the ambulance and direct the crew to take her to the hospital immediately. It was some consolation that they would have done that very thing, had her life or that of the baby been in danger.

He sat down beside her on the wide step of the ambulance, hooking an arm around her shoulders and pulling her against his body. And he watched and waited.

As dawn broke across the water-washed street, Draco stirred. Satisfied with her breath sounds, the ambulance officers had left some time earlier and Draco had managed to coerce Blair into waiting in the limousine for the fire department to finish.

Under the cold, spreading light of sunrise, the true devastation of the building became clear. Charred beams hung at drunken angles from the ceiling, roofing iron in scorched twisted ribbons falling to what remained of the restaurant floor. The air was still thick with the stench of destruction, rancid with the fight of the flames against the firefighters' defense.

There would be an investigation, Draco had been told, and even though the building was insured and Blair had insurance to cover loss of business, the stark impact of the smoldering, sodden, charcoaled ruin that had been her livelihood rammed home with a finality that no one could deny.

Blair got out of the car as the fire department cordoned off the remnant of what had been her home and her life. Deep shudders rocked through her body. There was nothing left. Absolutely nothing. Her legs began to buckle beneath her, but strong arms closed around her, lifting her off her feet and carrying her back to the limousine.

She didn't even have the energy left to protest. What

was the point? Every last thing that had mattered to her was irrevocably burned to the ground.

Draco took her back to his apartment and she dragged in a breath of the sea air as they got out of the car. But still the scent of burning dreams remained lodged in her nostrils. She made no protest as he guided her to the elevator that sped them upstairs to his penthouse suite, and was docile as a baby as he stepped into the shower with her, both of them fully dressed, and began to peel away her clothes under the warm flow of water.

He tossed their wet clothes out of the shower door and they fell in a sooty, sodden mess she was too tired and broken to care about. With tender hands Draco shampooed her hair and rinsed it out before repeating the action, then with a soft cloth and liquid gel soap he gently washed her whole body until the water pooling around her feet ran clear.

Once she was clean, he switched off the water, dried her and dressed her in one of his oversize T-shirts, then slid her between the cool cotton sheets of his bed. Then and only then did Blair allow her mind to let go of the horrors of the night, and let sleep claim her.

Blair woke hours later to the drone of male voices from the other room. Her throat still felt raspy, and she gratefully reached for the bottle of water that Draco had no doubt placed at her bedside while she slept. As she let the deliciously clear liquid slide down her throat she heard Draco's voice.

"And the baby? The baby will be all right?"

He must have called a doctor. She listened as the

voices grew more distant, and then heard the faint sound of the front door being opened and closed.

She sank back against the sheets, feeling more lost and alone than she ever had in her entire life. The baby was still his primary concern. Yes, she knew it should be hers too, but just for once, the little girl buried deep inside her cried, why couldn't it be her?

She cast a blurry gaze over at the bedside alarm clock and sat upright when she saw how late it was. Her father's surgery would be over by now. She was supposed to have been with him before he went in, and then later when he was moved from recovery.

Blair swung her legs over the bed and put her feet on the floor, but before she could stand Draco was there at her side.

"Can I help you? Do you need the bathroom?"

She shook her head; she didn't need his solicitous behavior. It wasn't as if he truly cared about her, anyway.

"No," she said, her voice rougher than usual, "I need to get to the hospital to see my father. He'll be worried."

Draco gently pushed her back down onto the bed.

"Your father has come through his surgery with flying colors, you don't need to worry. And the surgeon explained to him why you couldn't be there. He's sleeping now, and I have one of my people there to let us know the minute he wakes. If you're up to it, I'll take you to see him myself."

Blair allowed him to lift her legs and tuck them back under the covers. Then, to her surprise, he sat down on the bed next to her.

"We can rebuild, you know," he said softly.

"Rebuild? The restaurant?"

An image flashed in her mind of the carnage the fire had wrought. It would take a hell of a lot to rebuild. A lot of money and time, neither of which she had at her disposal. But then again, she didn't own the building, did she? Draco did.

She remembered what she'd said to him as he'd arrived at the scene and had the grace to blush. She'd been overwrought. Why on earth would he do something as destructive as set fire to his own building? She wanted to apologize, but the words stuck in her throat.

"Yes, the restaurant. There are many photos of the exterior. We could rebuild, using recycled timbers wherever possible, and remain true to the original building. It will be better than before. We can ensure that it has all the charm of the old restaurant, but with all the convenience and functionality of a new one. What do you say?"

"Is that what you want to do?" she asked tentatively.

"How can it not be what I want, Blair, when it is so important to you?"

He took both her hands in his and lifted them to his mouth, the softness of his kisses to her knuckles making her feel cherished. The sensation was foreign to her. All her life she'd had to be responsible. To look out for herself. But this, this felt surprisingly like being looked after. Warmth bloomed deep inside her.

"Blair, I cannot explain to you how I felt when I arrived back in Auckland and heard of the fire. They said there were casualties, but I had no way of knowing if it was you they were talking about. That journey from the airport was the longest of my life. And then, when I got to the restaurant, I couldn't see you anywhere. To be honest, it was a relief to see you come at me with all your accusations."

"I'm sorry. I was upset, crazy. I should never have said those things to you."

Of course he'd been relieved to see her. After losing Marcella and their unborn babe, he would have been frantic about this child. Her heart ached with wanting even a fraction of that care to have been about her—just for herself.

"Don't apologize," Draco said, letting go of her hands and getting up to pace the room. "It is I who should apologize. I treated you as if I were some feudal overlord and you nothing more than one of my serfs. I saw you. I wanted you. It was that simple. And when I discovered you were pregnant with my baby, Blair, I was prepared to do anything and everything to keep you."

A glimmer of hope kindled to life in Blair's shadowed soul. Could he have feelings for her that went beyond the physical attraction that drew them together, that even now simmered beneath the surface?

"I was unfair to you when you asked about Marcella. To be honest, it pained me to talk about her. Not for the reasons I imagine you're thinking. Yes, I loved her. Who could not? But was I in love with her? Did my sun rise and set with her? Did I spend every waking moment of every day after I met her looking forward to when we could be together again?" He shook his head disparagingly, his face drawn into sharp lines of self-contempt.

"No, I did not. And she deserved that. She deserved someone who would love her every second of every day. But instead, she loved me. And because she loved me she destroyed her life to give me what she believed would tie me to her in a way she never could. She allowed herself to become pregnant, knowing how dangerous that was, to make me love her more.

"I have lived with the guilt of knowing that for too long, Blair. I didn't believe I deserved to love or to be loved. Not after being so cavalier with Marcella's feelings, with her love for me.

"But then I met you, and instantly you brought light into my life. Suddenly I found reasons to work from home. You remember, *si?* When you first arrived at the palazzo with your tour, I was on my way out the building, but I saw you get off the tour bus and it was as if I was hit by lightning. I wanted you in that instant, and I still want you—even more than I did back then."

"How could I forget?" Blair answered in a whisper.

Listening to Draco talk about their first meeting was like reliving the exquisite sensation of being instantly desired all over again.

"I thought that I was being given another chance," Draco said, his voice so low she could barely hear him. "But you were only supposed to be with us that day. When you agreed to stay, I couldn't believe my luck. My world began to spin on a new axis, up until you left again. You were so focused on your work, on Carson's, that I couldn't begin to see how I could tempt you into staying with me forever. Instead, all I could see again was what my life could be like. It was as if fate was playing a cruel joke on me by giving me what I so justly deserved. I'd taken Marcella's love for me for granted and poured myself into my work, and suddenly, even though I didn't realize yet that what I felt for you was love, you did exactly the same to me."

Blair pressed her hand to her heart. If for one moment she'd known the depth of his feelings, could she believe she might have acted any differently? She had probably been so damaged by her father's slant on love and his own obsession with his work, not to mention her own painfully failed relationship with Rhys, that she would not have been open to a permanent overture from Draco. Not then.

"Draco, I think you're being too hard on yourself. How could Marcella not have loved you? You're strong, successful and so handsome it makes me ache deep inside whenever I see you. And your heart, your passion for all that you love, is like a drug that makes those around you want to be part of that love—part of you.

"You terrified me and drew me like a magnet at the same time. But because of you, I've learned an awful lot about myself that I wasn't prepared to see before. And I've learned to identify exactly what my greatest hopes and dreams are—"

"Carson's," Draco interrupted her sitting back down on the bed beside her. "I will rebuild it for you. I promise you Blair. If that's what it takes, I will do it for you."

Blair reached out and pressed her fingers to his lips. "No. That's not what I want. Sure, I thought Carson's was my be-all and end-all. What else did I have to dream and strive for in my life? No, I've learned that Carson's was my father's dream and his alone. I absorbed his hopes and dreams as my own when I had nothing else, exactly as he did when my mother left him. It was easier to pour all those feelings into work than into setting himself up for failure again with other relationships, and believe me—he failed often.

"I think seeing that example in my life showed me that you can have control of something in your life. What you do, if not what you feel. By default, his dreams became my own. But you know, deep down inside, I always wanted what he never had—a partner to stand by me, through anything and everything. Someone to love me and be loved by me in return. But it was so much easier not to take the risk. Loving hurts. It leaves you open and vulnerable and requires the utmost trust to commit to."

She leaned forward and pressed her lips against his.

"I don't want to be like my father and drive myself so hard for something that it eventually destroys my life, and I don't care if you don't rebuild Carson's. It doesn't matter to me, not anymore."

"What *does* matter to you?" Draco asked, as he tilted her chin so she looked him straight in the eye.

"You. You and our baby and the life we can have together, if you'll have me. Draco, I love you. I've fought it tooth and nail, but I can't deny it any longer."

"*Cara mia,* never doubt it. I love you more than I ever believed a man could love a woman. I don't ever want to lose you. You and only you are the love of my life— my reason for being—and, if you'll let me, I want to spend the rest of my life with you. Growing old with you. Loving you."

Blair wrapped her arms around Draco's neck and drew him closer to her. "Then start now," she said softly against his lips. "Show me."

Draco pushed aside the covers of the bed and gently coaxed her against the pillows. His fingers skimmed her arms, her legs, before gently lifting the hem of the T-shirt up and over, until she was exposed before him—naked, but for the cloak of love that swathed around them both.

Her body thrummed with desire, but this time it felt different, as if they were finally in perfect tune with one another. And when he removed his clothing and settled his body over hers she knew what made that difference. It was the absolute security of knowing she was safe with him, that she had offered him her heart and that she knew at a level that went soul-deep, that he would cherish and protect that gift for all of his days.

And as their bodies slowly began to move in unison, Blair knew that she would do the same for him.

Forever.

* * * * *

Don't miss the last Rogue in Yvonne Lindsay's
ROGUE DIAMOND *series,*
PRETEND MISTRESS, BONA FIDE BOSS
available April 2009 from Silhouette Desire.

*Celebrate 60 years of pure reading
pleasure with Harlequin®!
Silhouette® Romantic Suspense is celebrating with
the glamour-filled, adrenaline-charged series*
LOVE IN 60 SECONDS
*starting in April 2009.
Six stories that promise to bring the
glitz of Las Vegas, the danger of revenge,
the mystery of a missing diamond, family scandals
and ripped-from-the-headlines intrigue.
Get your heart racing as love happens
in sixty seconds!*

Enjoy a sneak peek of
USA TODAY *bestselling author Marie Ferrarella's*
THE HEIRESS'S 2-WEEK AFFAIR
*Available April 2009 from
Silhouette® Romantic Suspense.*

Eight years ago Matt Shaffer had vanished out of Natalie Rothchild's life, leaving behind a one-line note tucked under a pillow that had grown cold: *I'm sorry, but this just isn't going to work.*

That was it. No explanation, no real indication of remorse. The note had been as clinical and compassionless as an eviction notice, which, in effect, it had been, Natalie thought as she navigated through the morning traffic. Matt had written the note to evict her from his life.

She'd spent the next two weeks crying, breaking down without warning as she walked down the street, or as she sat staring at a meal she couldn't bring herself to eat.

Candace, she remembered with a bittersweet pang, had tried to get her to go clubbing in order to get her to forget about Matt.

She'd turned her twin down, but she did get her act together. If Matt didn't think enough of their relationship to try to contact her, to try to make her understand why he'd changed so radically from lover to stranger, then to hell with him. He was dead to her, she resolved. And he'd remained that way.

Until twenty minutes ago.

The adrenaline in her veins kept mounting.

Natalie focused on her driving. Vegas in the daylight wasn't nearly as alluring, as magical and glitzy as it was after dark. Like an aging woman best seen in soft lighting, Vegas's imperfections were all visible in the daylight. Natalie supposed that was why people like her sister didn't like to get up until noon. They lived for the night.

Except that Candace could no longer do that.

The thought brought a fresh, sharp ache with it.

"Damn it, Candy, what a waste," Natalie murmured under her breath.

She pulled up before the Janus casino. One of the three valets currently on duty came to life and made a beeline for her vehicle.

"Welcome to the Janus," the young attendant said cheerfully as he opened her door with a flourish.

"We'll see," she replied solemnly.

As he pulled away with her car, Natalie looked up at the casino's logo. Janus was the Roman god with two faces, one pointed toward the past, the other facing the future. It struck her as rather ironic, given what she was doing here, seeking out someone from her past in order to get answers so that the future could be settled.

The moment she entered the casino, the Vegas phenomenon took hold. It was like stepping into a world where time did not matter or even make an appearance. There was only a sense of "now."

Because in Natalie's experience she'd discovered

that bartenders knew the inner workings of any establishment they worked for better than anyone else, she made her way to the first bar she saw within the casino.

The bartender in attendance was a gregarious man in his early forties. He had a quick, sexy smile, which was probably one of the main reasons he'd been hired. His name tag identified him as Kevin.

Moving to her end of the bar, Kevin asked, "What'll it be, pretty lady?"

"Information." She saw a dubious look cross his brow. To counter that, she took out her badge. Granted she wasn't here in an official capacity, but Kevin didn't need to know that. "Were you on duty last night?"

Kevin began to wipe the gleaming black surface of the bar. "You mean during the gala?"

"Yes."

The smile gracing his lips was a satisfied one. Last night had obviously been profitable for him, she judged. "I caught an extra shift."

She took out Candace's photograph and carefully placed it on the bar. "Did you happen to see this woman there?"

The bartender glanced at the picture. Mild interest turned to recognition. "You mean Candace Rothchild? Yeah, she was here, loud and brassy as always. But not for long," he added, looking rather disappointed. There was always a circus when Candace was around, Natalie thought. "She and the boss had at it and then he had our head of security escort her out."

She latched onto the first part of his statement. "They argued? About what?"

He shook his head. "Couldn't tell you. Too far away for anything but body language," he confessed.

"And the head of security?" she asked.

"He got her to leave."

She leaned in over the bar. "Tell me about him."

"Don't know much," the bartender admitted. "Just that his name's Matt Shaffer. Boss flew him in from L.A., where he was head of security for Montgomery Enterprises."

There was no avoiding it, she thought darkly. She was going to have to talk to Matt. The thought left her cold. "Do you know where I can find him right now?"

Kevin glanced at his watch. "He should be in his office. On the second floor, toward the rear." He gave her the numbers of the rooms where the monitors that kept watch over the casino guests as they tried their luck against the house were located.

Taking out a twenty, she placed it on the bar. "Thanks for your help."

Kevin slipped the bill into his vest pocket. "Any time, lovely lady," he called after her. "Any time."

She debated going up the stairs, then decided on the elevator. The car that took her up to the second floor was empty. Natalie stepped out of the elevator, looked around to get her bearings and then walked toward the rear of the floor.

"Into the Valley of Death rode the six hundred," she silently recited, digging deep for a line from a poem by Tennyson. Wrapping her hand around a brass handle, she opened one of the glass doors and walked in.

The woman whose desk was closest to the door

looked up. "You can't come in here. This is a restricted area."

Natalie already had her ID in her hand and held it up. "I'm looking for Matt Shaffer," she told the woman.

God, even saying his name made her mouth go dry. She was supposed to be over him, to have moved on with her life. What happened?

The woman began to answer her. "He's—"

"Right here."

The deep voice came from behind her. Natalie felt every single nerve ending go on tactical alert at the same moment that all the hairs at the back of her neck stood up. Eight years had passed, but she would have recognized his voice anywhere.

* * * * *

Why did Matt Shaffer leave heiress-turned-cop
Natalie Rothchild?
What does he know about the death of Natalie's
twin sister?
Come and meet these two reunited lovers and learn
the secrets of the Rothchild family in
THE HEIRESS'S 2-WEEK AFFAIR
by USA TODAY bestselling author
Marie Ferrarella.
The first book in Silhouette® Romantic Suspense's
wildly romantic new continuity,
LOVE IN 60 SECONDS!
Available April 2009.

CELEBRATE
60 YEARS
OF PURE READING PLEASURE
WITH HARLEQUIN®!

Look for Silhouette®
Romantic Suspense in April!

Love In 60 Seconds

Bright lights. Big city. Hearts in overdrive.

Silhouette® Romantic Suspense is celebrating
Harlequin's 60th Anniversary with six stories that
promise to bring readers the glitz of Las Vegas,
the danger of revenge, the mystery of a missing
diamond, and family scandals.

Look for the first title, *The Heiress's 2-Week Affair*
by *USA TODAY* bestselling author
Marie Ferrarella, on sale in April!

His 7-Day Fiancée by **Gail Barrett**	May
The 9-Month Bodyguard by **Cindy Dees**	June
Prince Charming for 1 Night by **Nina Bruhns**	July
Her 24-Hour Protector by **Loreth Anne White**	August
5 minutes to Marriage by **Carla Cassidy**	September

REQUEST YOUR FREE BOOKS!

**2 FREE NOVELS
PLUS 2
FREE GIFTS!**

Passionate, Powerful, Provocative!

YES! Please send me 2 FREE Silhouette Desire® novels and my 2 FREE gifts (gifts are worth about $10). After receiving them, if I don't wish to receive any more books, I can return the shipping statement marked "cancel". If I don't cancel, I will receive 6 brand-new novels every month and be billed just $4.05 per book in the U.S. or $4.74 per book in Canada, plus 25¢ shipping and handling per book and applicable taxes, if any*. That's a savings of almost 15% off the cover price! I understand that accepting the 2 free books and gifts places me under no obligation to buy anything. I can always return a shipment and cancel at any time. Even if I never buy another book, the two free books and gifts are mine to keep forever.   225 SDN ERVX 326 SDN ERVM

Name	(PLEASE PRINT)

Address	Apt. #

City	State/Prov.	Zip/Postal Code

Signature (if under 18, a parent or guardian must sign)

Mail to the **Silhouette Reader Service:**
IN U.S.A.: P.O. Box 1867, Buffalo, NY 14240-1867
IN CANADA: P.O. Box 609, Fort Erie, Ontario L2A 5X3

Not valid to current subscribers of Silhouette Desire books.

**Want to try two free books from another line?
Call 1-800-873-8635 or visit www.morefreebooks.com.**

* Terms and prices subject to change without notice. N.Y. residents add applicable sales tax. Canadian residents will be charged applicable provincial taxes and GST. Offer not valid in Quebec. This offer is limited to one order per household. All orders subject to approval. Credit or debit balances in a customer's account(s) may be offset by any other outstanding balance owed by or to the customer. Please allow 4 to 6 weeks for delivery. Offer available while quantities last.

Your Privacy: Silhouette Books is committed to protecting your privacy. Our Privacy Policy is available online at www.eHarlequin.com or upon request from the Reader Service. From time to time we make our lists of customers available to reputable third parties who may have a product or service of interest to you. If you would prefer we not share your name and address, please check here. ☐

SDES08R

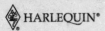

COMING NEXT MONTH
Available April 14, 2009

#1933 THE UNTAMED SHEIK—Tessa Radley
Man of the Month
Whisking a suspected temptress to his desert palace seems the
only way to stop her...until unexpected attraction flares and he
discovers she may not be what he thought after all.

#1934 BARGAINED INTO HER BOSS'S BED—Emilie Rose
The Hudsons of Beverly Hills
He'll do anything to get what he wants—including seduce his
assistant to keep her from quitting!

#1935 THE MORETTI SEDUCTION—Katherine Garbera
Moretti's Legacy
This charming tycoon has never heard the word *no*—until now.
Attracted to his business rival, he finds himself in a fierce battle
both in the boardroom...and the bedroom.

#1936 DAKOTA DADDY—Sara Orwig
Stetsons & CEOs
Determined to buy a ranch from his former lover and family rival,
he's shocked to discover he's a father! Now he'll stop at nothing
short of seduction to get his son.

#1937 PRETEND MISTRESS, BONA FIDE BOSS—
Yvonne Lindsay
Rogue Diamonds
His plan had been to proposition his secretary into being his
companion for the weekend. But he *didn't* plan on wanting more
than just a business relationship....

#1938 THE HEIR'S SCANDALOUS AFFAIR—
Jennifer Lewis
The Hardcastle Progeny
When the mysterious woman he spent a passionate night with
returns to tell him he may be a Hardcastle, he wonders what a
Hardcastle man should do to get her back in his bed.

SDCNMBPA0309